Stone Dreams

A Novel-Requiem

Central Asian Literatures in Translation

Series Editor
REBECCA RUTH GOULD (University of Birmingham)

Editorial Board
ERDAĞ GÖKNAR (Duke University)
JEANNE-MARIE JACKSON (Johns Hopkins University)
DONALD RAYFIELD, PROFESSOR EMERITUS (Queen Mary University of London)
ROMAN UTKIN (Davidson College)

Other titles in this series:

Farewell, Aylis: A Non-Traditional Novel in Three Works
Akram Aylisli
Translated by Katherine E. Young

Night and Day
Abdulhamid Sulaymon o'g'li Cho'lpon
Translated and introduced by Christopher Fort

https://academicstudiespress.com/calit

ACADEMIC
STUDIES
PRESS

Stone Dreams

A Novel-Requiem

AKRAM AYLISLI

Translated by
KATHERINE E. YOUNG

Boston
2022

Translation of this manuscript was funded by a 2017 Translation Fellowship from the National Endowment for the Arts.

Library of Congress Control Number: 2022938878

ISBN 978-1-64469-913-3 (paperback)
ISBN 978-1-64469-914-0 (PDF)
ISBN 978-1-64469-915-7 (ePub)

Academic Studies Press
1577 Beacon Street
Brookline, MA 02446, USA
press@academicstdiespress.com
www.academicstudiespress.com

Dedicated to the memory of my fellow countrymen,
who left us their unwept pain

Table of Contents

Foreword: Stone Dreams and Akram Aylisli's Life of the Mind

Every day an elderly writer sits in his apartment a few blocks from the Caspian Sea and reads—but only a little, as his eyesight is poor.

His preferred reading is fantastical and satirical novels such as Don Quixote and Mikhail Bulgakov's *The Master and Margarita*. He recently completed his own translation of another favorite, Salman Rushdie. While he can step out of his apartment and walk down to admire the blue-gray sea, his physical world is limited to these streets.

Indeed, this writer's life now resembles that of a surreal tale by his favorite authors. At the age of 84, Akram Aylisli is an outcast. He cannot leave the capital of Azerbaijan, Baku, or visit his native village. He is isolated from old friends, family members, and readers. His books have been burned and pulled from Azerbaijan's libraries, theaters, and schools. Mostly what remains, he says, is the life of the mind.

"For many years now, my only salvation from the dirt of the outside world is literature," Aylisli told me. "There is more air for me there than in the whole city of Baku."

If the Azerbaijani government's tactic has been to cut Aylisli off from the world, they have largely succeeded. In 2016 the writer, then aged 78 and already in poor health, had been preparing to fly to speak at a literary festival in Venice. But at Baku airport, he was detained by Azerbaijani police officers for allegedly assaulting a border guard. Five years on, prosecutors have still done nothing to substantiate this bizarre charge (which technically means the case should be closed), and Aylisli's travel and identity documents remain confiscated.

The dethroning of Aylisli, formerly the national writer of Azerbaijan, happened overnight in 2013. Protestors burned Aylisli's effigy and held up a symbolic coffin outside his apartment block in Baku. In Azerbaijan's second city, Ganje, a crowd built a pyre and threw his books on it. His Belarussian-born wife was sacked from her job as director of a children's library. Both of his two sons lost their job and one left Azerbaijan.

Since then, Aylisli, his wife, and his son have spent almost all of their hours in their small Baku apartment, a few meters from the British Embassy, with little to do, suffering from a kind of physical and political cabin fever. We corresponded in the summer of 2021, and I visited him in February 2022, just as Russia had invaded Ukraine. The writer's mood, already gloomy, was made even darker by the new war. "Satan has appeared," he remarked as we sat in his living room.

Why is Aylisli being punished in his own homeland? He had broken the central taboo of modern Azerbaijan when he published the novella published here in Katherine E. Young's excellent English translation—*Stone Dreams*.

To understand the importance of *Stone Dreams* and why its publication created such a storm, some background is needed on the Armenian-Azerbaijani conflict over Nagorny Karabakh. Since the late 1980s, this has been a conflict at least as toxic as the Israeli-Palestinian dispute, consuming Armenia and Azerbaijan almost entirely. In the early 1990s, fighting over the disputed mountainous territory of Nagorny Karabakh claimed 20,000 lives and forced more than a million people to flee from their homes. Each republic was almost entirely cleansed of the population of the other.

Official discourse allows no light and shade. In Azerbaijan, Armenia is presented entirely as an aggressor and occupier of Azerbaijani lands. Armenians routinely decry Azerbaijanis as inherently "genocidal" and barbaric. In reality, as in most ethno-territorial conflicts, both sides have committed crimes against the other, from the pogrom that killed peaceful Armenians in the Azerbaijani city of Sumgait in 1988 to the massacre of Azerbaijani civilians outside the village of Khojaly in 1992. And yet, for long periods in their history, Armenians and Azerbaijanis have lived together harmoniously and share many common elements of culture and tradition. Everyone knows this, but very few in either country dare to say it out loud. Aylisli's is the clearest voice.

On 27 September 2020, the Armenian-Azerbaijani conflict restarted, ending an imperfect ceasefire that had lasted 26 years. Over 44 days, the Azerbaijani military, with military assistance from Turkey, upended the defeats and losses the country had suffered in the war of the 1990s. They recaptured land that had been under Armenian military control for decades. As a result, thousands of Karabakh Armenians fled ahead of the Azerbaijani advance, before a Russian-brokered truce took effect in November.

Azerbaijan reaped humanitarian benefits: its victory will potentially allow hundreds of thousands of its citizens, displaced in the 1990s, to return home. But the human cost of the war was huge. More than 7,000 Armenians and Azerbaijanis died, most of them young soldiers who were not even born when the first Karabakh war was fought. Hatred and trauma were kindled in a new generation, as reports came in of prisoners summarily executed and schools bombarded. Armenian and Azerbaijani social media overwhelmingly became platforms of hate and disinformation.

Since the ceasefire of November 2020, the situation has remained volatile, raising prospects of both war and peace. One thing unfortunately has not changed, especially on the Azerbaijani side: angry and triumphalist rhetoric.

Space for peacemakers is limited, though growing a little. For years Aylisli's voice was drowned out by the noise, though he still hopes that his book *Stone Dreams* has had some influence. "By the publication of Dreams I saved many Armenians from hatred towards Azerbaijanis. I am proud of that and will be proud forever," he said.

Path from the village

Before 2013, there were only a few clues in Akram Aylisli's biography that the writer would take such a stand.

He was born Akram Naibov in 1937. His father, a soldier in the Red Army, died when Aylisli was five, and the future writer grew up in poverty. He comes from the village of Aylis in Nakhichevan, the remote exclave of Azerbaijan which borders Armenia, Iran, and Turkey. Once he became a writer, he adopted the nom de plume Aylisli ("Akram of Aylis") in honor of his home.

"The important thing to understand is that he grew up in a village," Shura Burtin, a Russian journalist who has championed Aylisli both as a writer and a peacemaker, told me from St. Petersburg. "He grew up in a different world," said Burtin, suggesting that his humble rural background conferred on Aylisli his distinguishing quality of "clarity," both moral and artistic. His home village of Aylis "is a huge character in all the books," concurs Katherine E. Young, Aylisli's English translator. She compares Aylisli's recurring writing about his village to the literary strategy of William Faulkner, using one place to be "both minute and broad in the scope of what he writes."

Aylisli studied in Moscow in the 1960s, during Nikita Khrushchev's post-Stalin "thaw." He was one of a group of writers from village backgrounds who wrote about rural life, breaking with the diktat to write socialist realist literature with boiler-plate heroes. His early works, especially a series of novellas entitled People and Trees set in Aylis, earned him hundreds of thousands of readers in his native Azerbaijan and also in Russian translation. Aylisli single-handedly "created the lyricism of Azerbaijani prose," says Jamil Hasanli, Azerbaijani historian.

Young notes how he marked himself out early by rejecting the patriarchal traditions of the Caucasus. Having lost his father as a child, he was brought up by women, and in his work his women characters are some of the strongest characters.

The dramatic topography and tragic history of Aylisli's homeland of Nakhichevan was also formative. Its high mountains descend to the broad Arax river, which runs for 1,000 kilometers between four countries. In the early twentieth century, Nakhichevan had a mixed Armenian-Azerbaijani population. In 1915-16 the Armenians of the Ottoman Empire were killed or deported in the Genocide, the worst atrocity of the First World War. Then, after the Russian Empire fell apart, Armenians and Azerbaijanis pitched into conflict. The briefly independent states of Armenia and Azerbaijan fought over Nakhichevan. After World War I, the Allied Powers briefly tried to make it a neutral protectorate. The Bolsheviks made it part of Soviet Azerbaijan in 1921.

The village of Aylis, which Armenians call Agulis, had a dozen Armenian churches and a large Armenian population as well as many Azerbaijani Muslims. In December 1919 Azerbaijanis and Turkish militias massacred most of its Armenian villagers. The burned ruins of the Armenian church of Aylis were the backdrop to Aylisli's childhood, but few talked about what had happened. An exception was his mother. "All my conscious life I carried compassion within me for the Armenians because, in very early childhood, my mother—a deeply pious Muslim—told me almost every day of the hideous atrocities which the Turks had committed in 1919," Aylisli wrote to me.

In the Gorbachev era, this memory suddenly became relevant as Armenians and Azerbaijanis revived old quarrels and violence broke out again. In 1989 Aylisli wrote a public letter to his colleague, Sergei Baruzdin, editor of the journal Druzhba Narodov (Friendship of Peoples), condemning the new nationalism and advocating dialogue. In the letter he confessed to feeling a "suffocating loneliness," as so few other Armenian or Azerbaijani intellectuals shared his stand.

After Azerbaijan became independent, Aylisli made an accommodation with the new regime. In 2005 he was elected to parliament as a deputy from his home region. Writing to me, he responded to the charge that he sold out by saying that both before and during his tenure in parliament, he wrote to Heydar Aliyev, Azerbaijan's president from 1993 (and before that, its Communist Party boss) and to Ilham Aliyev, Heydar Aliyev's son and successor, speaking out against human rights abuses and the systematic destruction of Armenian historical monuments in Nakhichevan.

The historian Jamil Hasanli, who later became one of the leaders of Azerbaijan's opposition, was also a parliamentarian at this time. Hasanli remembers that during a break in sessions, he found Aylisli looking downcast. "'Is something wrong?' I asked him. Aylisli responded by saying, 'You know, our government is dead, our parliament is dead, the intelligentsia is dead, we are also dead.' I tried to cheer him up a bit and said, 'But you are one of the most alive people in the country.' He laughed and said: 'I'm also dead, I just died quite recently.'"

All this time, Aylisli was secretly working on the novella *Stone Dreams*. In 2012 a new scandal erupted. At a NATO training course in Budapest in 2004, Ramil Safarov, a young Azerbaijani officer, had brutally murdered an Armenian classmate and was given a long jail sentence. In a deal between Hungary and Azerbaijan, Safarov was returned to his homeland, only to be pardoned, set free and lauded by much of the Azerbaijani establishment as a "hero." As international criticism rained down on Azerbaijan for this grotesque act, Aylisli evidently decided his dissenting voice needed to be heard. He sent *Stone Dreams* for publication in Moscow at the end of 2012.

The novella is set at end of the year 1989, as Armenian-Azerbaijani violence escalates. The main protagonist, the actor Sadai Sadygly, comes, like Aylisli, from the village of Aylis; unlike the real Akram Aylisli, however, the character intervenes with more than words to counter violence. After being beaten by a mob for defending an Armenian, he is admitted to hospital in a coma. In flashbacks we learn how Sadygly is obsessed with the 1919 massacre of Armenians in Aylis and eventually decides to become a Christian as expiation. His skeptical wife rebukes him for forgetting the suffering of his fellow Azerbaijanis.

In Azerbaijan, the publication of the novella—or reports of it, as few actually read the Russian text—came like an explosion. Aylisli was vilified as a traitor by everyone from the president downwards and stripped of his state literary awards and special pension.

"He was not a fighter before, but suddenly he performed this brave deed," said Shura Burtin. It seems he felt he must finally dissent from the path his country had taken.

The author says he is proud that *Stone Dreams* caused a stir, but he also maintains that his text was misunderstood. Sadygly, he says, is a "highly vulnerable person of high morals, who is on the edge of psychological collapse." In the text itself, the author compares him to Don Quixote, the arch-defier of reality.

Damned in Azerbaijan, *Stone Dreams* was celebrated in Armenia—and also misunderstood, some say. Armenian writer and journalist Mark Grigorian said that much of the Armenian public—very few of whom also read the actual text—merely concluded that an Azerbaijani writer had apologized to them, proving the Armenian cause was just.

"I think *Stone Dreams* is more about the hero's conversation with God," Grigorian said, who reads it as a deeper reflection by the writer on why evil has befallen his region.

Aylisli's bold call was to put Armenian-Azerbaijani symbiosis at a higher level than the nation-building project of either country. The call was heard, but mostly unanswered. "The book is directed to [Armenian] intellectuals, I believe the intellectuals understood the message, this book shouts that it needs someone, a writer from the Armenian side, to respond," Grigorian remarks. Some of them did respond, he says, but Armenia lacks an author with the same combination of literary talent and the status of "conscience of the nation." (The writer who came closest to fitting that description was actually a contemporary and friend of Aylisli, Hrant Matevosian, but he died in 2002.)

Aylisli says that he has no desire to exculpate Armenians for their actions in the conflict. "They acted criminally and stupidly when they seized seven whole regions around Nagorny Karabakh," he wrote to me. "And it cost them dearly." In the essay Farewell Aylis, which ends the English edition of his work, he reserves some of his caustic criticism for Armenian writer Zori Balayan, blaming him, it seems, not just for his nationalist messages which helped ignite conflict, but for compromising his vocation as a writer.

Having found a new voice, Aylisli had more in store. He wrote a novella, titled A Fantastical Traffic Jam, a straight-out political satire, with little of the pastoral lyricism of his other works. Its protagonist, a grasping official named Elbey, falls out of favor with the all-powerful "Master," the leader of a post-Soviet republic named Allahabad, and loses everything.

A Fantastic Traffic Jam was published in a small edition of just 50 copies, to test his friends' reactions—one copy of which duly fell into the hands of the all-seeing authorities. Several commentators have speculated that this book was actually a bigger sin in the eyes of the Azerbaijani leadership than *Stone Dreams*. In it, Aylisli lifts the lid on the corruption and craven behavior in the inner circles of an authoritarian regime. He spares no one, for example a state-sponsored singer of whom he says, "it was impossible to doubt his love for the Glorious Allahabad Party, love that had cost at least fifteen thousand dollars." This is the sum, we are told, that the singer receives in cash in a sealed envelope every time he sings songs glorifying the leader.

Reclaiming memory

The new Armenian-Azerbaijani conflict has left Aylisli more isolated, even as the Nagorny Karabakh conflict remains unresolved and an alternative voice like his is needed even more urgently.

But Aylisli has no illusions as to why the authorities are keeping him so isolated—to wait for him to die. "For a long time I have had no doubts that they have a pre-agreed plan to keep me in this situation to the end of my life," he wrote to me.

A banned author, whose books were burned, Aylisli risks being forgotten. PEN International has campaigned for him, but he remains a writer in a country few people know, who does not speak English, and does not seek out publicity. Yet there is an appetite to read and hear him.

An online event organized by the Harriman Institute of Columbia University in December 2020 attracted hundreds of participants, many from the younger generation thirsting to hear someone who had so radically broken with the dogmas of nationalism surrounding the conflict. Yet Aylisli, a self-confessed technophobe, admits that his arm was twisted to appear live. He answered questions fluently for an hour, but seemed relieved to take a cigarette break when moderators gathered questions.

In Azerbaijan, few have backed him publicly. Aylisli told me that he has received messages of support—mainly from older Russian liberal writers, naming, amongst others, Boris Akunin, Andrei Bitov, and Viktor Yerofeyev.

Katherine E. Young, his translator, enthuses about Aylisli's early work and wants to see it published in English. What is for sure is that the more non-Russian speakers get to read his books—and to grasp that he is not just a civic activist, but a remarkable writer with a 50-year track record—the more readers and supporters he will receive. To read *Stone Dreams* as some kind of political tract is to negate its importance as a work of literature.

To hear Aylisli talk, it is as though conflict has cast an evil spell over the Caucasus and struck its inhabitants dumb:

> We had so much that it was good when we were together. But for some reason everyone has decided to keep silent about that. It's as though some kind of mysterious catastrophe occurred: people's memory vanished in a flash. But it is memory that moves us forward in all our actions. But now it's as though everyone has decided to live without memory.

Thomas de Waal

Translator's Note

The 2012 Russian-language publication of Azerbaijani writer Akram Aylisli's novella *Stone Dreams* (*Daş yuxular* in Azeri, *Kamennye sny* in Russian) rocked the world of Azeri- and Russian-language letters. As Thomas de Waal recounts in his introduction to this volume, reaction from the government of Azerbaijan was swift and brutal. Almost a decade later, author Akram Aylisli remains under threat of legal proceedings and cannot leave the city of Baku, where he has lived under de facto house arrest since 2013.

Stone Dreams is the second work in a trilogy of novellas set in late-Soviet and post-Soviet Azerbaijan. The novellas trace themes of regional history (both ancient and modern), nation building in the post-Soviet era, corruption, moral cowardice, the limits of the individual human spirit, and the enduring power of art. The full trilogy, *Farewell, Aylis*, is available in English from Academic Studies Press. *Farewell, Aylis* also contains an afterword by author Akram Aylisli, in which he describes watching his books burn in his beloved hometown of Aylis and recounts his hopes for eventual reconciliation between Armenians and Azerbaijanis, one of the threads that runs through all these novellas.

Stone Dreams has never appeared in an authorized public edition in Azeri, the language in which it was originally written; Akram Aylisli himself translated it into Russian for its 2012 publication in the Russian journal *Druzhba narodov*. I translated *Stone Dreams* from that Russian-language version, in consultation with Mr. Aylisli. Rebecca Ruth Gould, Central Asian Literatures in Translation series editor for Academic Studies Press, provided invaluable guidance in rendering personal names, place names, ideas, and ideologies originally conceived in Azeri, Armenian, Persian, Russian, and other languages, cultures, and political environments—some of them extending back into ancient history—into accessible English. Margarit Ordukhanyan graciously assisted with terms that originated in Armenian. Any remaining errors are my own.

Although some of the organizations and individuals who have materially and otherwise supported this project cannot be publicly named, I am profoundly grateful to them all. I am particularly grateful to the U.S. National Endowment for the Arts; to Shura Burtin and Natasha Perova in Russia; to Harold Leich at the Library of Congress; to Umair Kazi and the Authors Guild; to Faith Wilson Stein, formerly of Academic Studies Press, for initially championing the project; to Alex Zucker and Marian Schwartz for sage advice; to Anne Harding Woodworth for her friendship and warm support; to Lisa Hayden for her remarkable insight into the mysteries of translation (including the mysteries of this translation); to Liza Prudovskaya, who read every word (sometimes many times over), and without whom this translation could never have been completed; to Daria Pokholkova at Academic Studies Press for carrying the project over the finish line; to Matthew Charlton at Academic Studies Press for spearheading this new edition of *Stone Dreams*; to Richard Kauzlarich and Thomas de Waal for their continued attention to this writer and his plight; and to John Williams and Alexander Young-Williams for their patience and good humor when duty called.

This translation is dedicated to the memory of Alexander Woronzoff-Dashkoff, teacher.

Katherine E. Young
27 March 2022

Stone Dreams

A Novel-Requiem

The Curious Death of an Old Coat Check Girl, the Deadly Dangerous Joke of a Famous Artist, and the Party Card-Pistol

The condition of the patient just delivered to the trauma department of one of the major Baku hospitals was very serious.

They took the patient, who was lying unconscious on the gurney, along the very middle of the half-lit hospital corridor that stretched the length of the whole floor to the operating room, which was located in the other wing of the building. There were two women in white lab coats and two men, also in lab coats. The surgeon himself walked beside the gurney, a spare, silver-haired man of middling height, distinguished from his colleagues by his reserve, the compelling sternness of his face, and the particular cleanliness of his lab coat.

If there was anything unusual or seemingly incongruous in this ordinary scene of hospital life, it was the tragic humor in the appearance and behavior of the person who'd brought the patient to the clinic. That small, fidgety man of fifty-five to sixty whose small face was not at all in harmony with his enormous, round belly ran around the doctor constantly repeating the same thing over and over.

"Doctor, my dear Doctor, they killed him! Such a man, in broad daylight, they beat him, destroyed him. It's those *yerazy*, Doctor, *yerazy*. Five or six of those *yerazy*-boys who fled from Armenia! Those sons of bitches, those refugees simply don't respect people, Doctor, my dear Doctor. They don't recognize artists or poets or writers. Just call someone an Armenian—and that's it! Then they slam him to the ground and trample him like wild animals. They tear him to pieces, and no one dares get involved. I told them: 'Don't beat him,' I said, 'That man's not Armenian, he's one of us, a son of our people, the pride and conscience of the nation.' But who listens? They didn't even let me tell them my name. They kicked me so hard in the side that I almost died there, too. Right here, Doctor, in the right side. It still hurts badly now."

The doctor didn't really understand what the man who'd brought the patient was saying. Maybe he didn't want to understand. Maybe he wasn't even listening to what that fussy, funny man who'd knotted a yellow tie over a brown checked shirt was babbling without pause. However, an observant person might have noticed that the doctor from time to time smiled into his moustache. And not because every word, every gesture of the man who'd brought the patient rose to comedy. But, rather, because the light-haired man lying on the gurney was slender and remarkably tall. And it's possible that the contrast in appearance between these two reminded the doctor of the very saddest pages of the story of Don Quixote and Sancho Panza.

When they reached the doors of the operating room, one of the men wearing a white lab coat blocked the path of the funny man in the yellow tie.

"Let him in," said the doctor. "It seems he has something to say. Let him have his say."

Although the operating room was considerably smaller than the corridor, all the same it turned out to be a spacious room with a high ceiling and gigantic windows. The operating table standing directly in the center resembled the linen-covered gurney on which they conveyed the patient. The two men in white lab coats delivering the gurney that bore the patient lifted him, laid him on the table, glanced at the doctor for permission, and silently left the operating room.

"Peroxide!" said the surgeon loudly to the nurses, rolling up the sleeves of his lab coat. "Bring it here, wipe off his face." Looking at the patient covered in blood, he muttered an oath, and turning to the man's companion, he asked, "Who did this to him?"

"I already told you, Doctor: *yerazy*. Those bastard refugees arriving from Armenia. It wasn't enough to smash his face. They also knocked him to the ground like wild animals and began beating him in the stomach. It's a good thing, Doctor, that I arrived in time. I went out this morning to get some air in the city. I'm coming down from that cursed place they call the Parapet when I see five or six mustachioed scoundrels beating up a man at the edge of the fountain. And people just standing by and watching in silence. . ." Then he suddenly hesitated. His lips continued to move, but the words, it seems, died in his throat.

"There's no more peroxide, Doctor," said one of the nurses in an apologetic voice, as quietly as possible. (One of them was elderly, the other quite young.)

"There should be some alcohol," said the surgeon, without hope.

"No, Doctor. Everything we had was used up yesterday."

"Fine, clean him with water. Don't use too much manganese." The doctor washed his hands with soap at the sink standing in the corner of the room and then went up and stood in front of the operating table. "Take everything off of him. Leave only his underwear."

The patient—his face, nose, chin, the collar of his orange wool shirt, the lapels of his bluish jacket covered in scarlet blood—was lying so calmly on the operating table that it was as if his most evil enemy rather than he himself had been beaten up in the aforementioned Parapet Square. He was sleeping deeply, although frequent, harsh moans escaped from his chest. Not only did he sleep but, apparently, also dreamed, and it seemed that his dreams gave him great satisfaction.

While the women washed the dried blood off the patient's face, the doctor checked his pulse. When the nurses had stripped the patient, he began to examine him attentively, as if compiling a report for himself or dictating to someone.

"Put two stitches in his lower lip. No fractures noted in the area of the jaw. Two dislocations in the left hand at the elbow and wrist. Two fingers dislocated on the right hand: the thumb and middle finger. Severe muscle trauma in the left leg. A fractured kneecap in the right leg. No serious anomalies noted in the back, rib cage, or spine. No skull fractures observed." The doctor fell silent and again cursed angrily. "A concussion!" He said this loudly for some reason and in Russian, then pulled a handkerchief from the pocket of his trousers, slowly wiped the sweat from his brow, and added in Russian, "A brutal beating!"

After every word the doctor said, the face of the man who'd brought the patient reflected all his feelings, all his pain and suffering. With difficulty, he held himself together, so as not to burst out sobbing. When the doctor had finished his exam, the man's self-possession was also at an end. He wept violently, like an aggrieved child.

The eyes of one of the women in the white lab coats standing beside the operating table (the younger one) filled with tears. The elderly nurse was also upset and shook her head woefully. And the doctor was very sorry for the man. He began to calm him.

"There, there, this isn't good. . . It's nothing terrible. In fifteen days your friend will be like new, I'll make a beauty out of him." Lowering his head, he thought a bit and then again lifted his head and asked cautiously, "So, you say this man is Armenian?"

The eyes of our comic hero bulged in surprise.

"Really, you don't know him?! You don't know Sadai Sadygly? The pride of Azerbaijani theater! Our number one artist! You really don't know this great master, Doctor? You haven't even seen him on television? You've even seen me on television more than once, Doctor. Maybe you just don't remember—Nuvarish Karabakhly, a well-known actor of comic roles. Maybe you don't know me. I'm not offended by that. But there's no one who doesn't know Sadai Sadygly. You see, no one else in the world has played Hamlet, Othello, Aidyn, and Kefli Iskender like he has."

"I recognized you immediately," said the young nurse with unconcealed pride.

"I've often seen the two of you on television," said her elderly colleague, for some reason a bit coquettishly. "But Dr. Farzani isn't to blame. He lived more than thirty years in Moscow, and it hasn't been three years since he returned to Baku."

Understanding now why the doctor didn't recognize him or Sadai Sadygly, the artist calmed down at once. And that the nurses, having recognized them immediately, hadn't let on, Nuvarish Karabakhly put down to the fact that they'd certainly feared the information would have been poorly received by the doctor.

Nuvarish Karabakhly guessed that all his words had gone in one of the doctor's ears and out the other. Either the doctor had been too immersed in his thoughts or else he, Nuvarish Karabakhly, had been unable to find the necessary words in his nervous state. Therefore, he tried to focus as much as possible and resolved to recount everything that had happened on the Parapet again, more simply and basically.

"It was like this, Doctor: today I was walking around the city. What time it was, I can't say exactly—maybe ten, maybe eleven. On the Parapet there's a place with a fountain—you've probably seen it. And suddenly a terrible shriek came from there. As if someone was howling. It turns out it was an old Armenian. He'd gone out to buy bread, and there he fell into the hands of the *yerazy*. Right in his housecoat! And slippers. When I got to the place, the unfortunate man was already dead and had been thrown into the pool. But his eyes were open, Doctor, and he was looking straight at me. I personally didn't see how they killed him. But people who were there earlier said that at first they threw the Armenian into the pool, right into the frozen water. He was an old man, he couldn't stay in the water. He wanted to climb out. And those guys were standing at the edge of the pool, kicking him, until they kicked him to death. And Sadai Sadygly, God help him, always has trouble circling around his head. Otherwise, how could he have been the one to show up at that moment in that cursed place? He couldn't hold back, that's what happened! He's an artist, a humane person. His heart couldn't bear it. He ran to help. And how could those *yerazy* know who and what he is? They've just arrived, they're not from here. So they took him for an Armenian and attacked like wild animals. If I'd been just a minute later, they'd have sent him to join the old Armenian. But God spared him—he remained alive. I beg you, Doctor, save him. The life of that great person is now in your hands." With these pathetic words, the artist finished his speech.

The doctor hurried to start the operation. But it seemed that some necessary item was missing.

Besides, the story of the artist had apparently shaken him. He didn't see anything particularly unusual in the fact that the Hamlet-Othello-Kefli-Iskender lying unconscious on the operating table had been trying to save an old Armenian. In the doctor's opinion, anyone who considered himself a human being would have behaved the same way. However, the inhabitants of the city, as if they'd come to an understanding about it, were trying to steer clear of what's called humaneness. It seemed it was no longer even worth their while to pretend to be human beings.

Just ten or fifteen days previously in that same operating room, Dr. Farzani had performed a very complicated operation on an Armenian girl of fourteen or fifteen who, by God knows what miracle, had been brought to the hospital.

In the metro, where it's always full of people, a few Azerbaijani women had attacked her and, watched by hundreds of people, inflicted savage punishment. And just a few days before that, some poet-degenerate had burst into the hospital and beaten up a doctor who'd worked in the cardiology department for forty years, driving him out of his office just because he'd had the misfortune to be born Armenian. After that, not a single Armenian remained at the hospital—neither doctors nor members of the supporting staff. Some had hidden at home, some had left Baku forever.

"Numaish *muallim*, it's as the Persians say: *mesele melum est*, the issue is clear," the doctor said in a cheerful voice that was not at all in concert with his obvious bad mood, shifting his surgical instruments.

Nuvarish Karabakhly wasn't offended that the doctor had mangled his name (a person who'd lived more than thirty years in Moscow had full right to do that), but he didn't fail to correct him:

"Who is Nuvarish Karabakhly, Doctor?" he said. "An ordinary actor. Hundreds of Nuvarish Karabakhlys aren't worth the little finger of Sadai Sadygly. It would have been better if those scoundrels had beaten me in his stead."

"Is he also from Karabakh?" asked the doctor, checking the patient's pulse again.

"No, of course not, Doctor. I'm not from Karabakh either. Karabakhly is just my stage name—I'm originally from Kiurdamir. And Sadai Sadygly was born in Nakhchivan, a place in the Ordubad region, the village of Aylis. A very ancient village, Doctor, although I've never been there myself. They say at one time many Armenians lived there. It seems seven or eight of their churches are standing there to this day. Apparently, those Armenians were very smart, good people. And Sadai Sadygly is the kind of person, Doctor, that even if the world turned upside down, he wouldn't call white black. He's suffered for his outspokenness many times already, but he hasn't learned anything. In a couple of months he'll turn fifty, but he remains a ten-year-old boy. He says what's on his mind. He can't even occasionally be silent, even in such dangerous times. He says it's not the Armenians but we ourselves who are bad. And he isn't afraid. He says it everywhere, all the time, in the theater and in the tearooms."

Dr. Farzani, his eyes widening, looked in the patient's face, this time with a kind of special interest. It was as if he'd just now seen him for the first time. The women, who'd been preserving a dead silence, suddenly began whispering in a lively way about something. Farzani took Nuvarish Karabakhly firmly by the arm and, leading him to the door, said:

"Well, young man, there's nothing more for you to do here. Go sit in the corridor, rest. And if you want, go home, drink a shot of vodka as needed, and topple into bed. Then come back if you want to. This isn't cutting out an appendix, my friend. A full overhaul is necessary here, which will take three or four hours. Don't worry. Your friend will live. I'll make such an Othello of him that Desdemona will faint with joy."

With those words, the doctor escorted the artist into the corridor and closed the door behind him.

———

When the double doors of the operating room closed, Nuvarish Karabakhly suddenly felt acutely alone, as if the whole world remained there behind those closed doors.

The melancholy of the cemetery wafted over the long, half-lit corridor. The lights were off. There was no one around. The giant, double windows on the opposite wall of the corridor were veiled in gloom, not admitting light; either they were extremely dusty, or it was already dark outside.

In only one place—not far from the glassed-in balcony by the doors—was a bench visible. There was nowhere else in the corridor to sit. Nuvarish Karabakhly walked slowly along to the bench, feeling dizziness and approaching nausea. He'd been wanting a smoke for a long time, but he didn't even have the strength to shove his hand into his pocket and pull out the pack of cigarettes.

Approaching the bench, he saw two plaques attached, one above the other, on the wall by the door. On the upper one, "DEPARTMENT OF TRAUMA AND SURGERY" was written in big, black letters, and on the lower one, in smaller letters, "Farid Gasanovich Farzani, Surgeon, Head of Dept." The door to Dr. Farzani's office was open.

No matter how worn out Nuvarish Karabakhly was, no matter how much he wanted to sit down, he didn't seat himself on the bench by the door. It seemed that if he sat down now, he'd never be able to get up. He peered cautiously through the open door into the office: a desk, two old chairs, a sofa, a safe, a refrigerator, an old television, an electric tea kettle, a sink. He pulled his cigarettes out of his pocket, but again he couldn't make up his mind to smoke. Feeling nausea approaching even more strongly, he moved towards the window and, before reaching it, saw that a similar long corridor stretched out on the other side of the operating room. In contrast to this empty one where Dr. Farzani's office was located by the entrance, the other corridor had an abundance of windows, and the bluish doors of the rooms strung out along the corridor looked out on opaque, ash-colored windows.

A man with his leg in a cast was smoking by one of these windows, leaning on crutches. Near the open door of the farthest room stood an old woman with a bandaged hand. Besides these two, there was not another soul in the corridor.

Nuvarish Karabakhly lit the cigarette he'd been holding in his hand all this time, but at the first drag darkness fell on his eyes. Afraid he'd fall down, holding onto the wall, he forced himself along to the bench and sat there a long time while the mist that had been obscuring his eyes gradually dissipated.

The mist didn't disturb Nuvarish Karabakhly. He was used to it.

The thing he was most concerned about now was how to inform Sadai Sadygly's wife, Azada *khanum*, about what had happened.

Nuvarish had often been in Sadai Sadygly's home. And he knew where Sadai's wife worked. Azada *khanum* was probably still at work. But to stand up and get himself to where Azada *khanum* worked was almost impossible for Nuvarish at that moment. He was still considering how to tell her about everything. The best thing was to stay here and wait until the operation had concluded. Then, when the operation was over, the wounded Sadai bandaged and conscious again, it would be much easier to tell Azada *khanum* what had happened. (He'd forgotten that today was Sunday, and she wasn't at work.)

Nuvarish Karabakhly had been married three times, but on that night not a single person in the whole city waited for him.

He'd undertaken his first attempt to create a family when he was nineteen or twenty; he'd simply seated his beloved in a taxi and, without an engagement, without a wedding, and without a dowry conveyed her to his father's home. The lack of a wedding would have been acceptable, but Nuvarish's mother could in no way forgive the bride for having arrived at her husband's home without a dowry. After a month-and-a-half war with her mother-in-law, the young woman collected her things and left the house, never to return.

Also during Nuvarish's youth, when he still played only cameo roles at the theater, the living conditions of one of the most senior theater employees had been "bettered." The senior employee's damp basement apartment in Baku's Montina Village district was given to Nuvarish, where he'd lived for only nine months with his second wife, who died of lung cancer. Nuvarish Karabakhly's third wife, Julietta, had been a worn-down, thirty-six-year-old virgin, the daughter of one of the most eminent actors of the theater. For about five years they had no children. Then a son had been born. But when the child was not yet three months old, Julietta had once fallen sound asleep during his night feeding, and waking up, she found the baby had turned blue, suffocated between her breasts. Julietta couldn't forgive herself: the dead baby wouldn't be quiet, he cried and begged for milk. And the mother stopped eating, drinking, and sleeping. The poor thing didn't live even ten days after the death of her baby. She wasted away, burned out like a candle, and disappeared like a shadow—as if she'd never been.

For more than ten years now, Nuvarish had had a wonderful, two-bedroom apartment in the center of the city. Up until February of this year, he'd led a so what lonely but, compared to the present, calm, maybe even too-happy and comfortable life in it. And then fate played a trick on him—now Nuvarish Karabakhly tried to make use of his apartment only at night, and mainly because there was nowhere else to go. In his own home he knew not a minute of calm or sleep or rest. The reason was that one of the employees of Baksovet, the city hall, someone who worked in a minor but very lucrative post—a hefty, paunchy hulk of a man—had seized the next-door apartment of an old theater employee, the coat check girl Greta Sarkisovna Minasova. Greta Sarkisovna had received that apartment on the tenth floor, the highest floor of their building, the same day Nuvarish received his. And now that hulk had turned it into a real, actual brothel. All day noises and crashing resounded through the wall. The animal laughter and shrieks of experienced prostitutes and girls who were still young (just getting into the profession) and their authentic and feigned moans of pleasure drove him out of his mind, giving the artist no peace during the day and disturbing his sleep at night.

According to rumor, the hulk had been one of the richest people of Shusha. He'd appeared in Baku not long before, found work at Baksovet, and bought a four-bedroom apartment in a cooperative building next to Nuvarish's building. The man was shaped like a block. The amazing width of his back exceeded any standard frame. He had thick, raven-black hair; thick, black brows of the same color; a wide, generous moustache; and the bulging, empty, expressionless eyes of a crocodile. Even the first and last names of that man expressed cruelty and ungodliness to Nuvarish Karabakhly: Shakhgajar Armaganov. A curse on whomever had given that animal a name!

One morning when it had just turned light, noise rose from the courtyard: they said, "Listen, people, some Armenian woman threw herself off a balcony." The tiny, old woman's body of Greta Sarkisovna was just expiring in a large pool of blood, but the strange news was already going around the city that the Armenian woman who'd thrown herself off the balcony had left a letter of repentance before her death: "I hate myself for the crimes Armenians have committed. I despise my own people and therefore don't want to live in the world anymore. Karabakh belongs to Azerbaijan. Long live Azerbaijan!"

Neither then nor now did Nuvarish have any doubt that the "suicide" was the handiwork of that Shusha hulk. It was fully possible that Shakhgajar Armaganov himself had thrown Greta Sarkisovna off the balcony. The times were like that now. Go ahead, throw even a hundred Armenians a day off a balcony! And Muslims along with them. It's possible to easily erase any person from the face of the earth if there's no one standing behind him. And with each day, the artist became more afraid of the man from Shusha. There weren't any laws, now, no courts—one fine day he could easily take Nuvarish himself and throw him off a balcony and call it suicide. Who'd find it worthwhile to investigate his crime, who'd prove that that cold-blooded, ungodly, and ruthless Baksovet functionary was also a real-life criminal?

The cold, grey shock of the stress he'd experienced still hadn't left his soul, but the delicate, emotional insides of the artist were already blazing with hatred and anger. But how many times a day can you reiterate the same thing to a district policeman—be a man, have a conscience, close that brothel because soon the whole city will turn into one endless whorehouse—? For that reason, the artist had been more than once to see the head of the police, and he'd sent so many telegrams and letters to the district Party committee, the Central Committee, even Baksovet, that in the end he resolved that either there was no authority in the country, or else those people in authority were all on the same side as the executioner Shakhgajar Armaganov. And at the theater, he told everyone what had recently been going on in Greta Sarkisovna's apartment. Except he never said a single word to Sadai Sadygly about it. He considered that to be pointless because the man lived in his own world, his head stuck in the clouds. Besides, Nuvarish Karabakhly didn't want to drag a man in whose genius he believed with his whole soul into that filth.

Now, even during the hottest summer days, the artist closed all his doors and windows tightly, and God alone knows how many torments he endured each night while waiting for morning. During one of those terrible nights, he even made a resolution, no matter what it took, to equip himself with a pistol. With that request, he approached numerous acquaintances who worked in the police and the military enlistment offices.

However, his request elicited nothing but laughter from people who were accustomed to laughing just at the sight of him. And when the artist had already completely lost hope of arming himself and finding even some sort of peace in his own home, a well-known writer who'd had three plays presented in their theater had showed him (only two days ago) the simplest way. According to the writer, nowadays every member of the Popular Front had one or even several pistols. And with the help of "those guys," it was possible to buy not only a Makarov or Kalashnikov but even a real machine gun. And again, according to the credible writer, for such a famous artist as Nuvarish Karabakhly, it would be enough to simply go to the office of the Popular Front and whisper two words in the ear of the Head Bey.

He'd known the Bey for a long time and quite well. They'd drunk tea hundreds of times in various Baku tearooms on the Boulevard, in Molokansky Garden, on Azneft Square, and even when he'd had almost nothing in his pocket, he always tried to pay for tea himself.

And thus, on coming out of his apartment building today at noon, the artist had headed straight for the office of the Popular Front. The Bey hadn't yet arrived. The artist stood around for about an hour near the office entrance waiting for him. Then he left to eat some breakfast in a café near the movie theater Araz; he drank a shot and a half of vodka and ate two servings of wieners. And when, coming out of the café, he again headed for the office of the Popular Front, there—near the pool with the fountain—he'd found himself involved in this terrible story.

Now, sitting on the bench in the hospital corridor and waiting for the end of the operation, Nuvarish Karabakhly dreamed up a wonderful scene in anticipation of his still-unrealized meeting with the Head Bey.

"Hello, Nuvarish Bey! I'm infinitely delighted to see you!" Thus (in the artist's fancy) the Head Bey affectionately and amiably greeted his longtime friend from the tearoom. "How are you, my dear fellow? What's new in the theater? Whose play are you staging? Just yesterday I was asking the guys about you. 'Something's up,' I said, 'he's not around. Find out where he is, why our master of the stage isn't around. Maybe he's in need of something?'"

Hearing "in need," the artist began laying out his request for the desired pistol. He was also intending to tell the Bey about the actively functioning brothel in the neighboring apartment, but the Bey, with the great sensitivity inherent in great people, already understood exactly what had led his old friend to the office of the Popular Front and generously delivered him from discomfort.

"It's really nothing, Nuvarish Bey!" Here, the Head Bey lightly stroked his beard. Then he announced loudly and enthusiastically, "It's our responsibility to protect people who are needed by the nation." After that, he lifted his telephone receiver and ordered someone, "Bring the artist a new pistol. This is my friend. Our great artist. Yes, times are tough, it's a dangerous period. As much as possible, we must protect our best people." The Head Bey (in the artist's fancy) pronounced exactly these words and, smiling affectionately at Nuvarish, quietly added into the receiver, "Throw in some extra ammo."

Finally believing that he'd soon receive a pistol from the Head Bey himself, Nuvarish Karabakhly remembered sadly how only a year and a half ago the two of them had long and pleasantly sat in various tearooms. He remembered May of 1979, when the then-First Person of all Azerbaijan had suddenly visited the theater and just as suddenly allotted him an apartment in the center of the city. He remembered how, back at the end of the 1960s, he'd once been plastered and, heading to the bus stop completely drunk, had met the person whom the people called the Master on the corner of Zevin Street. At that time Nuvarish Karabakhly still lived in his father's house and had just begun to go on stage at the theater in cameo roles. However (there are indeed miracles in the world!), it turned out that the then-Master had seen these minor roles of Nuvarish. And not just seen, but vividly remembered.

That night the Master was also returning, it seems, from some kind of party and was in excellent spirits. (There were two strong men walking right beside him—bodyguards.)

"Oh, Artist, wait up, brother," he said. "Well, you've been drinking! Where did you get so sloshed?" He winked at one of the men standing next to him. "I've been drinking, too. Only, look, the earth isn't wobbling on its axis."

At that time Nuvarish wasn't formally acquainted with the First Person in the Republic, naturally, and if the First Person hadn't stretched out his hand and said, "Pleased to meet you," he probably wouldn't have remembered whom he'd run into that night on the corner of Zevin Street.

"Pleased to meet you," said the First Person, giving his name. "And you I know, you're an artist. And play good roles in the theater. And where are you going now?"

Nuvarish, stumbling over his tongue, stammered faintly, "To Khy-Khy-Khyrdalan. I'm taking the bus."

The man with the slightly oblong face scanned the artist from head to toe.

"Well, go!" he commanded with frightening disdain. "It's already late. At a march! And don't drink so much again."

"Do you still live in Khyrdalan?" Those words, spoken years later in the theater by the First Person, sounded so alive now in the ears of the artist that it seemed even the lifeless walls of the hospital corridor heard them clearly.

"Now I live in Montina Village—one floor underground," the artist had joked boldly with his longtime acquaintance.

"From tomorrow, you'll live in the center of the city—on the tenth floor above ground," the First Person said firmly, answering the joke with a joke.

That night, having performed Akhundov's *Monsieur Jordan*, the whole creative collective of the theater gathered in the office of director Maupassant Miralamov. In the show Nuvarish played the dervish Mastali Shakh, and his performance, to all appearances, was pleasing to the First Person himself. "You also play Sheik Akhmed in *Corpses* extremely well," he said. "I've seen it twice on television. Play those kinds of roles more."

It was clear that day that while getting ready for the theater, the Master had planned in advance to bestow apartments on several employees, among the lucky number of whom necessarily must have been Greta Sarkisovna Minasova. "There was one elderly employee here—Minasova. Does she still work in the theater?" the Master had asked the director for the sake of form, knowing, of course, that she never left the theater for anything. And Greta Sarkisovna, losing her head after the unexpected invitation, had walked into Maupassant's office whiter than a corpse, but came out crying from happiness and repeating over and over, "Thank you, my son! Thank you so much!!!"

To this day, Greta Sarkisovna's face on that night stood before the eyes of the artist. Maybe it was even more alive now than then, still more expressive. And also Sadai Sadygly's face turning grey, his eyes reddening, his glances full of fury and anger.

For some reason, he hadn't hit it off with the First Person from the very beginning. However, in Nuvarish's opinion the fault lay not with the First Person but in the stubbornness and pride of Sadai Sadygly. "He makes friends by dishing out delicacies from the common pot—our common pot—as if it were his own. He gives everyone something, taking away the most important thing in a man—his dignity. He castrates the soul of the people so as to make everyone quiet and obedient." Sadai Sadygly wasn't afraid to pronounce similar terrible words even in the presence of the theater bosses.

"So, are you in need of anything, Mr. Sadygly?" Speaking in a constrained and uncertain voice that didn't sound like his own, the First Person had then turned to Sadai, and it seems his voice even shook a little with those words. But open sarcasm and even hidden anger sounded in the word "Mr." Of course, the "mindset" of Sadai Sadygly was well known to the First Person. "I don't need anything!" Sadai Sadygly answered, loudly and loftily. When speaking with the First Person, everyone always rose. But Sadygly didn't even stir. "When he doesn't have anything better to do, he comes here to have some fun. He gives out apartments to everyone with such largesse—apartments owned by the state!—it's as if all the buildings in the city had

been left to him by his late father," he said angrily in front of everyone at the end of the gathering, not afraid of anyone. The next day
everyone in the theater was saying with regret that if Sadai Sadygly
had behaved himself a little more "decently" in the presence of the
Master, then he, too, would have been given an apartment in the
center of the city, in the very best building, whose apartments were
not even accorded to some of the ministers.

After that, just try saying that the tongue isn't the most despicable enemy of man.

Finding room for himself in a corner of the bench and curl-
ing up into a ball, Nuvarish Karabakhly fell asleep, and the artist
dreamed what was, perhaps, the most nightmarish dream of his life.

It was a strange, greyish place. Dampness penetrated to the
bone. There were no buildings, no trees, no one and nothing in
the world except a black puddle of blood. Like a small turtle just
hatched from the egg and hurrying towards water, Greta Sarkisovna
crept out of the pool of her own blood. Her naked body with its
raw skin, dead and at the same time living, was so ugly and terrible that perhaps no one since the creation of the world had seen
such a terrible sight. Greta Sarkisovna crawled and crawled across
the earth, wriggling like a snake. However, this wasn't the asphalt
courtyard of the building where Nuvarish now lived. This place
resembled the naked earth in Nuvarish's Khyrdalan courtyard, and
Greta Sarkisovna crawled across that earth, trying, it seems, to crawl
to her death. But that death never came to her, exactly as if it had
been stolen and teasingly hidden away by someone. Sometimes,
lifting her head, she murmured, "Thank you, my son! Thank you
so much!" and in unbearable pain and torment again continued the
journey towards her death. And Nuvarish suddenly realized that
Greta Sarkisovna was crawling straight towards him. As if her death
were in the power of Nuvarish himself.

And Greta Sarkisovna wanted to receive death from him, so as to forever rid her raw body of torment and suffering. The closer Greta Sarkisovna crawled, the greater the fear and horror that enveloped Nuvarish. The artist tried to run from the dead woman who was unable to die. However, he wasn't able to do anything—he couldn't move a single inch. It was as if his whole body had been bathed in molten lead.

Unable to bear the nightmare, the artist opened his eyes and—happy—came to himself in the cold and damp corridor. The lights were already on, and the operating room doors at the other end of the corridor stood wide open.

When Nuvarish Karabakhly, not yet fully recovered from the dream, entered the office of Dr. Farzani, the doctor immediately understood he was in no shape even to talk.

Farzani had just left the operating room. He stood at the sink with his face to the wall and washed his hands.

"Come in, sit down, Mubariz *muallim*," he said. "Don't worry. Things are going well. Your friend's in a room. Fast asleep. His constitution is strong. Made of iron, really. Just between us, he certainly doesn't look like much of a drinker."

In his state, the artist didn't even notice that the doctor had called him Mubariz and not Nuvarish.

"What do you mean, Doctor? What do you mean 'asleep'? He's conscious now?"

"Not yet," answered the doctor calmly, wiping his hands. "Don't be in a hurry, everything in its own good time. If not tonight, then tomorrow morning, for sure, he'll come to himself. I assigned an excellent nurse to his room. She'll be in constant attendance on the patient until morning." The doctor hung the towel on a nail and sat down in his place. "And you, obviously, fell fast asleep, although you look pretty beat up. What, did you have a bad dream?"

"Indeed I did, Doctor, how did you guess? I've never had such a nightmare in my life!" The artist fell silent. Then, suddenly, he sobbed loudly, and through tears he began entreating the doctor, "For the love of God, Doctor, give me some rubbing alcohol, just one swallow! I'm suffocating, I swear to God. My head is just splitting. It's as if rats and mice are running around inside my skull."

"No, my friend, that won't do it," the doctor said gently, sincerely pitying the artist. He spread out an old newspaper on the desk. He locked the office door. From the refrigerator he took a small carafe that was misted over and contained some kind of transparent liquid, clear as a tear, and stood it on the desk. On the newspaper he spread out a bit of sausage. A couple of pickled cucumbers. The salty curd cheese called *shor*. Lavash baked on a *saj*. A bunch of cilantro, picked over and washed. He poured cornelian cherry vodka into two pear-shaped tea glasses. At just the sight of the vodka, the artist's eyes began to shine.

"You're a really good person, Doctor. As soon as I saw you, I understood that." The artist stretched his hand towards the glass, but he didn't touch it because the doctor hadn't lifted his glass. Dr. Farzani's glance was directed towards the sink. And the artist understood what the doctor meant by that. He washed his hands with soap, came back, and sat down.

"Shall we drink?" said the doctor with a smile and drank his vodka. He took a piece of lavash, picked up a bit of *shor* with it, and directed it towards his mouth.

"To your health, Doctor!" Nuvarish drank standing, winced, and sat down.

"Chase it down with sausage. Eat up," the doctor commanded his guest. However, he himself didn't touch the sausage. He took a pair of cilantro sprigs and slowly began to chew. "Does he have family?"

"He has a family, Doctor. He's got a terrific wife, Azada *khanum*. She's a splendid dentist and a good person. She's the daughter of Dr. Abasaliev, the well-known psychiatrist. Maybe you've heard of him?"

Now Dr. Farzani was completely surprised.

"Who doesn't know Dr. Abasaliev?" he said. "Is he still alive?"

"He's alive, Doctor. And doing quite well!" answered Nuvarish inspiredly, having come to himself after the vodka. "He's still sound, just like an ice ax. It's already been a year since he moved, and he's been living at the dacha in Mardakan. 'I,' says he, 'won't concern myself with crazy people any more. Now there are too many of them spread all over the place.'"

"So our friend is the son-in-law of Dr. Abasaliev?" asked the doctor, pouring vodka into the glasses again.

Nuvarish Karabakhly went into raptures because the doctor was pouring vodka and because he had now said not "your friend" but "our friend."

"Yes, yes, his son-in-law. Moreover, they're great friends. They simply adore one another. For more than thirty years they've been living together. Well, who else does Dr. Abasaliev have? His wife is gone. Only the one daughter remains. Thus, he treats Sadai Sadygly like a son."

"That's how it is. . ." said the doctor, thinking of something else. "And it seems that they're from the same place, is that right? As far as I know, Dr. Abasaliev must be from Nakhchivan. . . Well, let's drink." He lifted his glass, drank, and again chased it down with some lavash.

"Exactly! They're from Nakhchivan!" confirmed Nuvarish, tossed back the vodka, took a piece of sausage, and swallowed, almost without chewing. "They're from the same village, both from Aylis. And both of them love their village like crazy people. No matter when or where they get together, they only talk about Aylis. Once, they say, there were many Armenians there. And it turns out they—meaning the Armenians—lived with our Muslims in great friendship. Dr. Abasaliev praises those Armenians very highly. He says that kind of cultured, honest, hard-working people can't be found anywhere else in the world. I've often heard their conversations. When father-in-law and son-in-law start talking about Aylis, you want to move and spend the rest of your days there."

Dr. Farzani listened to the artist, continuing to think about his own concerns.

"So that means Dr. Abasaliev is in Mardakan now," muttered the surgeon as if to himself, then thought for a moment and asked, "Does he live there alone?"

"Of course, whom does he have left? But Azada *khanum* visits him often. Every Sunday morning she goes out there to him. She stays the night, and in the morning she goes straight from there to work. You're right, it's difficult for an old man to live at the dacha. However, he doesn't have much free time in which to get bored. In the apartment here he had over thirty thousand books. Poor Azada *khanum* has been dragging them from Baku to Mardakan for a whole year already. And Dr. Abasaliev just sits in the dacha and reads those books. They even say he has begun to write himself."

"And they don't have any children?"

"No, Doctor. On the one hand, of course, it's a good thing such a person as Sadai Sadygly doesn't have children. Honestly, this is a person who's not of this world. He's always somewhere up in the clouds. And his character is entirely childlike. When he was still little, out there in the village someone shot a fox cub in front of him. So, he remembers that cub to this day. He's told me about it many times. And every time he has tears in his eyes, that's the kind of person he is!"

"So, you say he's a good artist?" the doctor threw out, obviously for the sake of keeping the conversation going.

Here Nuvarish Karabakhly arrived at the highest state of excitement.

"He's a genius, Doctor, I swear to God! This is a great artist on the level of Abbas Mirza and Ulvi Rajab. And well educated, exactly like a scholar. What books he's read! But stubborn as the devil in his character. Indeed, he sorely loves to dig in his heels. He could've received the title People's Artist ten or twenty years ago. But to this day he remains, like me, an Honored Artist. Because he can't hold his tongue. In 'seventy-nine he and two other of our artists were recommended for the rank of People's Artist. The day before, everyone was congratulating him. But in the newspapers the next day they printed only the names of the other two, and there was nothing about him. It turns out that the night before he'd been drinking heavily with someone and again let his tongue run loose: says he, 'I don't need any rank of the kind that your generous Master gives out left and right—let me earn my rank in the eyes of the people.'"

The artist rummaged a long time in his pocket. Then, clearly, having willed himself to it, he extracted a single cigarette from the pack and looked imploringly at Farzani.

"Doctor, allow me just a single drag. Don't fuss at me, for the love of God. I desperately want to smoke."

The doctor took a small glass ashtray from the desk drawer and placed it in front of the artist.

"Smoke as much as you want. I smoked for exactly forty years, starting at age twenty-five. But I gave it up five years ago." He poured vodka from the carafe again. "Well, let's drink one more glass—and that's enough. A good thing, the purest thing, something that never did harm.

"I have an acquaintance from Qazakh. And he has an interesting name—they call him Aftandil. Once his car rolled over, he broke all his ribs. And I had to give him a thorough overhaul. Every time he comes here, he brings me a couple of bottles of vodka." The doctor opened the window a little, took his glass and, right there by the window, drained the cornelian cherry vodka. "So, then, you said he doesn't need any rank given out by the authorities? And who reported that to the Master in the middle of the night?"

"Someone obviously did, Doctor. Otherwise, why would they cross out just his name of the three?" Having smoked half his cigarette, the artist put out the stub in the ashtray. "For some reason, he hated the Soviet authorities from the very beginning. Believe me, he couldn't bear them. I think it was in 'sixty-eight. One of our shows was in the running for the State Prize. Five performers received it, but Sadai Sadygly was left out again. But you know, he played the lead role. Then, too, he simply couldn't reign in his tongue. He blurted out to one of the members of the Central Committee, right to his face, he says, 'That thing you've got in your pocket, it's not a Communist Party membership card, it's a pistol. You frighten people with your pistol—you control them with fear so you yourselves can live without fear.'"

Not yet having drunk his third shot, Nuvarish was already in such spirits, he was experiencing so much lightness and happiness in himself, that if it had been solely up to him, he would have burst into a jig. On the one hand, the vodka he'd drunk was affecting him but, on the other, there was the happiness that he was sitting and talking with such a great surgeon as Farzani. And all the torments he'd experienced over the course of the day, even the nightmare he'd had not long ago, were forgotten. Even that son of a bitch Shakhgajar Armaganov himself now seemed not quite so frightening to the artist. And Dr. Farzani was pleased with the refreshed, restored look of his artist guest.

"Come on, drink," the doctor ordered in a friendly manner. "So, a Party card-pistol! Well said. Bullseye! If you're not trying to scare someone, why does any of us need a Party card?"

Nuvarish drank the vodka, and this time he also decided to chase it down with lavash and *shor*.

"But why even bring up a pistol, Doctor? Sometimes he comes out with these things, I tell you, you wouldn't believe. Once, during a banquet in Nardaran, that village where they're so pious, they beat him up very badly—he found himself there at a circumcision celebration. And during that kind of banquet, you know, there are certain rules: if you're asked to speak, you have to speak according to those rules. And what should one say when celebrating a circumcision? That it's a thing pleasing to God, how important it is for hygiene and health. Talk about the saints and imams. About the teachings of the Prophet, where this rite is considered one of the most important for Muslims, about His great wisdom... And at the very height of the banquet, Sadai Sadygly is asked to speak as an honored guest. And yet again something comes over him. He starts to mock the rite. Then he gets completely worked up, forgive me, Lord, he begins to insult the Prophet himself. 'Is it possible,' he says, 'that your Prophet is smarter than God? If there were something unnecessary in the body of a person, would God really be so blind as not to see it? How could it be that the Lord, not having made a single mistake in creating the face, eyes, nose, and ears and having done everything else correctly, suddenly, the devil knows how, came to this part where he up and made a mistake like a schoolboy? Who commanded your Prophet to correct God's mistake?'

"Never in their lives had the Nardaranians heard such a thing. And what happened next! The village elders bestowed every kind of curse there is on Sadai. Even the women, who didn't sit at the table, yelled from behind the fence, 'A curse on you!' In the end, when the banquet was finished, the youth of Nardaran thrashed him soundly. They beat him so badly, poor devil, that he was then unable to go on stage for three whole months. They say that Sheikh Allahshukur Pashazadeh, the head of all the Muslims of the Caucasus, personally visited Sadai in the hospital to persuade him to publicly apologize before all the Nardaranians. Because the offended Nardaranians might easily have killed him afterwards."

The artist recounted this tragicomic story with delight and even, of course, with a little embellishment. Suddenly he looked at the doctor, noticed the expression of his face had entirely changed, and was frightened that it had been too much for him. It seemed to the artist that the doctor had disliked his story very much. Therefore, he hurriedly and uneasily added:

"How should I know, maybe none of that even happened. Maybe some idiot like me, a clown worse than me, just made it up." And he fell silent, deeply upset and evidently having decided that the deadly dangerous joke of Sadai on the God-fearing Nardaranians had also offended the religious feelings of Dr. Farzani.

But Farid Farzani wasn't a fanatical Muslim. The doctor didn't observe the fasts, didn't perform the prayers. However, living in Moscow he'd tried as much as possible to follow the rules and laws established by his religion and the Prophet.

And the faithfulness to his religion that had remained more or less intact in him was precisely the main reason for Farid Farzani's sudden move from Moscow to Baku. If, just three years ago in Moscow, someone had told him that the artist now lying unconscious in his hospital room had once slandered the Prophet, it would have required a great deal of strength for the doctor to listen to that. However, what he'd seen during three years in Baku had sharply changed his attitude towards religion and towards his motherland and towards the Prophet himself. The doctor had been especially struck by the brutality of the Muslim population of the city towards Armenians, possibly because he personally had never seen similar brutality on the part of the Armenians.

"Is the sheikh also from Nakhchivan?" the doctor asked thoughtfully, obviously preoccupied and dispirited.

The question surprised the artist.

"Of course not, why? The sheikh's from Lankaran, he's an ethnic Talysh. And he seems to be a good person, gentle." The artist was silent a while, seeking the right words. "To tell the truth, I'm uncomfortable asking. But you yourself, Doctor, who are you by birth? Your last name seems to be Iranian."

"And I'm Iranian." The doctor sighed deeply. "My father once did something foolish and brought me here. And I myself did something even more foolish—I moved here from Moscow. I worked as a surgeon for fifteen years in the Sklifosovsky Hospital." The doctor pronounced the last few words with special pride, again poured a little vodka in the glasses, and added, "Let's drink to the health of our atheist. Let's hope he won't fall into the hands of savages again." And for the first time, the doctor clinked his glass with Nuvarish.

The artist increasingly felt a liking on the part of the surgeon and like a child rejoiced wildly at that.

"Yes, yet, let's drink to it, Doctor, let's hope he doesn't fall into the clutches of savages like those unfeeling *yerazy* again. But, Doctor, his wife had a presentiment of this long ago. She knew something like this would happen to him someday. And she tried to arrange it so that her husband never went out in the street. And he didn't go out. Except he went to the theater for a couple of hours last night. I myself phoned him from the director's office and just barely convinced him to come. Because he also grew tired of the theater. He didn't come even to pick up his salary. God alone knows why he happened to be in the city today."

"Smoke, go ahead, smoke." Doctor Farzani decided to deliver the artist, who'd again been rummaging in his pocket, from torment. He went up to the half-open window and flung it wide open. "Such a person can hardly continue to live in this city," he said with a shaking voice and, hunching his shoulders, lost himself in thought.

Yes, the artist had observed correctly: the mood of Dr. Farzani had really changed unexpectedly. And not because weariness had suddenly fallen on him or because for some reason he hadn't liked the artist's story. The fact is that at one time the doctor himself had heard the words spoken by the artist at the celebration of the circumcision from his own wife: "Your Prophet is wiser than God, is he?" At the time, they'd rocked Farid Farzani. And because of them his wonderful family in Moscow had fallen apart. Those exact, offensive words that had deeply wounded him were the reason for his present single and joyless life in this essentially foreign city.

At times fate brings astonishing gifts: married to a Russian woman, not having experienced the slightest psychological discord during many years in Moscow, the happy father of an only daughter, Farid Farzani all of a sudden began to lose his peace of mind after the birth of his son. When the son was still a baby, the question of circumcision had already turned into a real problem for the father. And that problem grew in proportion to the son's growth. Persistent unease led the doctor to start having nightmares, something that had never happened to him before. One morning when the son turned twelve, Farid Farzani expressed his firm resolution to his wife: "Such law is decreed by the Prophet. I don't have the right to break it."

And on hearing "Your Prophet is wiser than God, is he?" from his wife, he could have beaten his head against the wall from fury.

That very same morning, after his wife had gone to work and his daughter to school, having easily persuaded his son, in just ten or fifteen minutes Dr. Farzani completed that which the Prophet considered the primary responsibility of every Muslim before Allah. Who would have thought that for an experienced surgeon of the Sklifosovsky Hospital that very simple operation could result in complications? However, whether from fright or some other reason, towards evening the boy's temperature spiked to 104 degrees. And the mother who, on returning from work, found her son in that condition lost the gift of speech in her stupefaction. She didn't say a word to her husband, didn't attempt to lower her son's temperature—just looked at the child in horror. Then she threw herself into the bathroom, taking shelter inside, and for a long time her weeping and sobbing could be heard from behind the locked door.

It turns out that the love of Russian women can very easily redirect itself into hatred. Although the boy got up the next morning and wandered calmly around the house, Farzani's wife broke off her relationship with her husband forever. She immediately filed for divorce and exchanged their three-room apartment in the center of the city for two two-room apartments in outlying districts. Having lived for several years without his family, in 1986 Farid Farzani traded apartments with a Russian in Baku, moved to Baku, and understood on the first day what an inexcusable mistake he'd made.

Now Farzani's son was nineteen. But in his father's memory, he remained a twelve-year-old. And for many years the innocent, bewildered eyes of the boy cruelly followed the doctor. The full horror lay in the fact that the boy, not having made a sound during the operation, later, when the doctor had finished what he was doing, looked at his father with such murderous contempt that it was impossible to forget that look. Farzani read in the boy's eyes that he would never forgive him for that operation. Only much later did the doctor begin to understand where the essence of his sin lay. It would have been all the same to the boy whether a piece of his foreskin or an entire finger had been cut off, because for a child brought up in Moscow circles, it was incomprehensible in whose name his father had acted thus. The boy perceived it as physical violence done to him on the part of his father, as utterly senseless cruelty and savagery. That morning the doctor clearly read in the eyes of the son spoiled and loved beyond all measure that he'd become a stranger to him.

And he comforted himself in vain with the idea that time would pass and the estrangement disappear. The father didn't have the strength to overcome it, and the son didn't even make the attempt. During the time Dr. Farzani had lived in Baku, his daughter had come to visit him twice. And now she phoned at least once a week, asked about his health, asked how he was doing. The son hadn't visited Baku once and didn't once phone.

Yes, the son was Dr. Farzani's weak spot. The story of the artist, apparently, had touched precisely that weak string, reopened the wound, and rubbed salt in it. He fell into a mystically melancholy mood completely uncharacteristic of him and tried in every way possible to come out of it.

"Yes, he's a born Don Quixote!" Farzani exclaimed with forced gaiety. "Don Quixote, that's a real role for him. When he recovers, I'll tell him that. What do you think, will he be offended?"

The artist looked at the doctor with surprise because he knew *Don Quixote* was Sadai Sadygly's favorite work of art.

"Tell him, why not." Agitated again, the artist once more stuck his hand into his pocket in search of a cigarette. "He's read *Don Quixote* a hundred times. Cervantes is his favorite writer. And among our authors he values Mirza Fatali Akhundov most of all. And among the living he has one idol, his father-in-law Dr. Abasaliev, and also some woman from his village, an Armenian named Aikanush, he always speaks of her with love." Nuvarish Karabakhly blurted out all this in a single breath and, dragging his hand from his pocket, looked meekly at the doctor.

Doctor Farzani had read *Don Quixote* at least two times and knew something about Mirza Fatali Akhundov, but about that Armenian woman Aikanush, of course, he couldn't know anything. On the other hand, he was well acquainted with Dr. Abasaliev. They'd met many times at various medical symposia in Moscow, Leningrad, Prague, Warsaw. . .

"And where does Dr. Abasaliev's daughter work?"

"At first she worked at the medical commission. But now a new dental clinic has opened on Neftianikov Prospekt, and Azada *khanum* works there." The artist looked at his watch. "Only she's not at work now. She's probably already home."

"But you said that on Sundays she goes to her father in Mardakan."

"Yes, she does. . ." Suddenly, it was as if a light had come on in the artist's head. "It's really Sunday today, Doctor, right?! My stupid brain forgot again, and all this time I've been tormented about how I'm going to go and tell Azada *khanum* about all of this. This is just great, Doctor. For the time being, let Azada *khanum* suspect nothing. But tomorrow, God willing, he'll be better, regain consciousness, and it won't be so difficult for Azada *khanum* to see her husband. They love one another so much. They don't have children, so they give one another the love they would have spent on children." Having said this, he looked at the desk from the corner of his eye. "Will you allow me to clear up?"

"Don't worry, they'll clean it up without you." The doctor carried the half-empty carafe to the refrigerator. "Do you have Azada *khanum's* telephone number?"

"Her work number, no, but I know their home number."

"Then write it down for me. Dr. Abasaliev probably has a phone at the dacha?"

"There's a phone there, but I don't know the number."

Dr. Farzani shook the artist's hand.

"Well, off you go, have a good rest tonight. But I have many things left to do."

"Doctor!" exclaimed Nuvarish Karabakhly, and he looked so mournfully at Farzani that he understood without a word what the artist wanted to say.

"We won't go into the room," he declared. "That's pointless. But don't you worry, everything's in order there. I gave him an excellent room, later you'll see for yourself and be sure of it. With a phone, a television—not a room but a khan's palace." Dr. Farzani looked at the paper with the telephone number that the artist had written for him. "And I'll get in touch with his family," he added, "Don't you worry about anything."

It was night, a cold December night in 1989. Nuvarish Karabakhly was very much afraid to go home. And it was precisely that fear that gave birth to a feeling of powerlessness and hopelessness in his soul.

If he'd been able to bring himself to do it, he'd have gone back to the hospital and asked for shelter for himself there, if only for one night; just a hospital bed in any old run-down room. The further he got from the hospital, the artist felt how an almost-physically experienced pain of loneliness was growing in him, and because of that, the evening he'd spent with Dr. Farzani had already turned into a distant, no longer attainable, pleasant recollection in his memory.

Dr. Farzani had charged one of those nurses who assisted him during the operation to sit by the bed of Sadai Sadygly—the seventy-year-old, experienced, long-serving Munavver *khanum*. The old hospital hands called Munavver *khanum*, who'd worked there more than fifty years, simply Mira *khanum*. A few called her Mina *khanum*. As for Dr. Farzani, what he called that experienced nurse who knew her business depended on his mood. In an ordinary mood, he called the grey-haired woman of approximately his own age simply Munavver or, familiarly, Sister. In a good mood, that indispensable colleague of the trauma department and surgery was always Minasha for him. And that special nickname gave Munavver *khanum* great joy every time she heard it.

It was the unwavering habit of Dr. Farzani to lock himself in his office and drink a couple of shots of vodka after every operation. When there wasn't an operation, the surgeon locked himself in his office towards evening all the same and for some time cut himself off completely from hospital life. He always drank in solitude; today was the first time he hadn't been alone in his office. For that reason, the nurse was quite worried. On the one hand, she was afraid that this time he'd drink more than his customary amount, and on the other, she was simply jealous; ordinarily, the doctor shared his solitude only with her.

And the meticulous and rule-following Munavver *khanum* was also worried that Dr. Farzani had given the order to place the patient in a room designated for those who were highest in the *nomenklatura*—a room that was under the personal control of the head doctor—and that perhaps the order had been given without the head doctor's approval.

"Here I am, Minasha!" That's how Dr. Farzani greeted the old nurse, coming into the room withhis white lab coat thrown across his shoulders. The warmth of that address, as always, was balm poured into Munavver *khanum*'s heart. Probably, she thought, Masha had phoned from Moscow, because only after a phone call from his daughter was Dr. Farzani so cheerful and happy.

"So, our artist isn't planning to return from the dead?" asked the doctor, taking the patient's pulse. "What a heart he has, Minasha. Beaten black and blue, and his heart works like a clock."

"Ah, Farid Gasanovich, if only you knew how he looked in his best years!" responded the nurse anxiously and sadly. "There were times when people went to the theater in droves just to see him on the stage. If only you knew how he played the role of Aidyn! It was so wonderful that even the men in the audience wept." The nurse, deeply moved, barely held back tears. "Do you see the kind of radiance that emanates from his face? And that's after so much torment! I just sit here, looking at him, I don't get tired of looking."

"Yes, a strong fellow," agreed the doctor, who left the bed of the patient and stood a little while by the window. Then he returned and sat in the armchair beside Munavver *khanum*.

"Only, Doctor," the nurse lowered her voice. "You should tell the head doctor that we put the new patient in this room. Just because that's the way it's done."

"I let him know," the doctor answered unwillingly and, getting up from the armchair, again went to the window.

It was as if a weight had lifted from the shoulders of the nurse. She quickly rose and moved towards the door at a brisk clip.

"I'll go clean up things in your office," she said, leaving, and then glanced again into the room. "Shall I bring you tea here?"

"Bring it here. Only don't forget to ask permission of the head doctor," answered the doctor, laughing.

After the departure of the nurse, the doctor again went to the window. He'd recently acquired this habit of standing by the window at night and looking at the deserted streets. It was strange that for several months already, not just at night but even during the day, it had been impossible to see people walking on the streets of Baku either alone or in pairs. Now people walked in crowds, herds. And the sovereign right to speak, shout, and extol was given only to these crowds. And it was stranger still that the quantity of words these beings cried out was probably equal to the quantity of words used when primitive people were on the hunt:

> *Free-dom!*
> *Re-sign!*
> *Ka-ra-bakh!*

In recent days, these people had enlarged their stock of words with two more phrases:

> *Death to Armenians!*
> *There you are!*
> *There you are!*

"There you are! There you are!" muttered Dr. Farzani to himself and walked away from the window.

On the yellowish face of the patient, he noted the clear trail of a tear that had rolled down one cheek.

O Almighty Lord, Be So Kind, Tell Me: Did You Create My Aylis or Did My Aylis Create You?

O Lord, what is this place?

Could this world of steps stretching from the steep bank of the river up along the slope of the mountain really have existed in Aylis? What on earth was that Aylis, where a single narrow gorge suddenly became enormous, like the world? Is it really possible that Aylis grew so great, or did someone collect all the steps carved of stone and all the ledges of the world and arrange them as far as the eye could see in that same narrow gorge of Aylis?

What is this place, O my God?

Perhaps it's the mouth of Babylon's Ishtar Gate in Mesopotamia. Or the Acropolis. Perhaps these steps and ledges lead straight up to the Parthenon. And why do these curved steps remind one so much of the stone seats in the theater of Dionysus?

Perhaps this stone world in the higher part of Aylis named Vuragyrd can be called Harmony. But for the moment it's impossible to say. Because from the stone ledge on which Sadai Sadygly stands, not a single stone of the church located in Vuragyrd can yet be seen. Besides, he'd come to this mysteriously wonderful world specifically in search of harmony, and if what the artist beheld was indeed harmony, then didn't his entire path beyond lose all meaning? In order to catch even a distant glimpse of that place towards which the artist was striving, he'd have to clamber up the stone steps for a long time still. But his legs refused to go, his hands wouldn't obey, and the heaviness in his head interfered with the movement of his body. As soon as the artist managed to climb just one step, then and there his strength deserted him. Then Sadai Sadygly would lie on the cold ledge, recover a bit, and again begin to move towards the majestic church built from hewn red stone that still wasn't visible. And each time he began to move, the ledges towering over him started to move, too. In this stone world made up of steps stretching from the bank of the river to the very heavens, the earth quaked, the ledges began to rock and shake, and along with that shaking and rocking stone world, Sadai Sadygly once more completely forgot where he was and what he was looking for, plunging into the absolute darkness of Nothing and Nowhere.

From the minute he'd lost consciousness, the artist had been in just this world.

When he'd left home that morning between eleven and twelve o'clock and headed towards the Parapet, a certain secret power had once more attracted the thoughts of Sadai Sadygly and again carried him to Echmiadzin, the ancient cathedral of the Armenian Apostolic Church. Sadai Sadygly had never been to Echmiadzin. However, recently almost every night in his dreams he'd walked towards it among steep rocks and cliffs, and in every one of those dreams, he wandered exactly halfway towards the Vuragyrd Church among the countless stone steps and ledges about which he'd read a great deal in books and seen in films.

The desire to set out for Echmiadzin—to accept Christianity with the blessing of the Catholicos himself, to remain there forever as a monk and beseech God to forgive Muslims for the evil they'd done to the Armenians—arose unexpectedly in Sadai Sadygly's soul on one of the nights after the events in Sumgait. And later Sadai Sadygly was unable to understand whether that wish had come to him in a dream or in waking life. However, on that morning he awoke filled with joy, washed, ate breakfast with gusto, drank tea with pleasure and, unable to hold back, excitedly shared this new, fantastic idea with his wife. Even without that, Azada *khanum* had recently been experiencing serious unease about the psychological state of her husband; she felt worried that day at work, and that evening she phoned Mardakan and, almost crying, told her father everything.

Dr. Abasaliev, having bid medicine farewell for good and having passionately collected all kinds of facts about the history of Aylis from various sources almost since his student days, supplied a diagnosis for his son-in-law without particular difficulty. "Manic-depressive syndrome," he said and, as if ashamed of the seriousness of his words, tried to turn it all into a joke. "He's, what, going there to circumcise the Catholicos? Let him go, don't stop him. Best case, he makes it to Vuragyrd."

And then, abruptly changing the subject, he began with youthful fervor to talk about his new enthusiasm. "Azia, yesterday I found the diary of a certain Armenian merchant in one of the books. That Zakary wasn't a very educated man, but he was an excellent merchant. And he kept a diary just so that merchants after him would know the main methods of trade. Azia, how that man loved Aylis! I'm simply astounded—do you know what Aylis represents for an Armenian? Why did they have to construct that heavenly corner among mountains overflowing with jackals and snakes, where there are a million times more stones than water and earth? Were there really so few places on earth for Armenians? I can't say why Echmiadzin is so widely renowned. In fact, I was there three or four times. However, now, in my old age, I understand that the true house of God is Aylis. In comparison with Aylis, that Echmiadzin is simply a sniveling youth. You tell Sadai that the Catholicos of Echmiadzin won't suit him in the role of teacher. Let him come here to his own teacher, who's more knowledgeable in the affairs of God," laughingly added Dr. Abasaliev.

"Stop it, Papa! You turn everything into a joke," said Azada *khanum* in a slightly irritated voice. "He experiences the fate of every Baku Armenian painfully, as if he alone is obliged to protect them from every attack. Each and every Armenian has become dearer to him than he himself. As if they're all heavenly angels, and we're just butchers thirsting for their blood. He thinks only of those Armenians of Aylis and just can't understand that today's Armenians aren't much better than our own brainless screamers. He simply can't forget the slaughter the Turks conducted in Aylis that he himself didn't see. It's you, Papa, who made him this way."

"No, my daughter, I've got almost nothing to do with this. From birth he was an honest, conscientious, and vulnerable person. And what today's Armenians are like is beside the point—the point is what we're like now. Sadai isn't interested in Armenians, past or present. He's only thinking about the ethnicity we share. Of course, you know how sincerely he loves his people—that's what distinguishes him from the ill-assorted, brainless screamers who've now multiplied around the world like mushrooms after rain." The doctor paused for a long time. Then he started speaking in the warm and tender voice his daughter knew exquisitely well. "You've read *Majnun and Layla*, my daughter.[1] Remember what Majnun does when the army of his tribe goes to the last assault against the army of the tribe of Layla's father. You know that war was started to punish Layla's cruel father, who didn't want to give his daughter to a person from another tribe. And Majnun, blinded by love for his Layla, pitying her father, at the decisive moment throws himself into helping the enemy army. Because that's what true love is. True love doesn't know any boundaries. You can love a woman that way, and also a motherland. That kind of love is a clear mirror, my daughter—only goodness and mercy are reflected in it. It doesn't come from life, but from God. That's what ails him, our Majnun. And how wonderful, my little girl, that the medicine to treat that illness still hasn't been found," concluded Dr. Abasaliev with tears in his voice, acknowledging his powerlessness in the situation.

Then Dr. Abasaliev lectured his daughter about Aylis for almost an hour on the phone. And that phone conversation not only didn't soothe Azada *khanum*, but increased her alarm still further. She was in utter dismay; it seemed to her that all the men around her were beginning bit by bit to lose their minds.

"Our church here in Vang is an exact copy of the one in Echmiadzin." Dr. Abasaliev had spoken those words at one time to his future son-in-law in the yard of the Vang Church. But how did the artist know that one of the many roads leading to Echmiadzin runs right through the Vang Church? In any case, length by length, inch by inch, he'd already surmounted that agonizing stone world consisting of steps and ledges that resembled Vuragyrd.

Oh, Lord, this is the one—the Vang Church. A yellow-rose sunbeam making its way through the crown of a cherry tree as high as a finely chiseled poplar fell on the very center of the stone cupola of the church and shone past it—not changing color or strength— on the crest of the mountain standing beyond. Once Sadai Sadygly, being in a fine disposition of spirits, had compared that light—first appearing, then slowly fading and disappearing from the church cupola and the crest of the mountain—to the smile of God and the radiance of the Almighty's eyes. God himself had sent that light. Without His blessing, how could Sadai Sadygly, currently uncon- scious in a Baku hospital, so closely, so distinctly see the Vang Church in Aylis, the yellow-rose light on its cupola, its yard, garden, and that same tall cherry tree disappearing as if it were a poplar into the height of the sky?

It was the start of the summer season. June 1952. The willows had already lost their bloom. Clusters of flowers still hung from the branches of the silver berry trees, from the jasmine and acacia. And there was also the pathway of mixed, multicolored flowers planted in front of the church by Aniko, whom everyone in Aylis called Anykh. And filling the heart with radiance, there was also the freshness of just barely blossoming sunflowers planted in the churchyard by Mirali *kishi*, who lived not far from the church and had turned God's home into his own private storehouse for firewood, hay, and straw.

It seemed as if the yellow-rose light on the high cupola spoke with the mountains—that were as high as it was—about the existence here, at one time, of the purity, sublimity, expanse, and beauty of the world. And Lyusik was present again in the yard of the most beautiful of the churches, the Vang Church: the artist Lyusik, granddaughter of Aikanush, a girl of thirteen or fourteen. That summer Lyusik had come from Yerevan for the first time to spend the summer holidays in Aylis, and from the very first day she didn't leave the churchyard from morning until night. But just how many times was it possible to draw one and the same church? Perhaps the church was just a pretext. Perhaps Lyusik also saw God's smile in the yellow-rose light that appeared morning and night on the cupola and believed she could draw it; perhaps she settled firmly in the churchyard, drawing exactly the same thing day after day, for that reason. And perhaps she already knew then that the church was an "exact copy" of the one in Echmiadzin. But for Sadai that knowledge lay ahead.

At that time, Sadai had never even heard the name of his future father-in-law.

It was a big event when, after many long years, Dr. Abasaliev appeared in Aylis with his daughter at the beginning of the 1960s. Sadai was studying at the institute in Baku.

At one time *Hajji* Hasan, the father of Zulfi—Zulfi, who became Dr. Abasaliev—had traded in Iran, Iraq, and Anatolia, and in Aylis he maintained his land, farm, cattle, and other property. *Hajji* Hasan heard about the Armenian-Azerbaijani hostilities in Isfahan, and returning to Aylis, he collected the most valuable possessions from his enormous holdings and moved his family to Baku for good.

When Dr. Abasaliev appeared in Aylis after many years, the upper story of their two-story house in the Muslim quarter had been almost completely destroyed. Only two rooms on the first floor were relatively well preserved. Putting one of them in order, Dr. Abasaliev began living there with his daughter, and at the same time he began to build a small, one-room house with a modest entry hallway for himself at the other end of the yard. With the active help of his fellow villagers, construction was finished in less than a month; he even managed to cover the roof with slate, which at that time was not found on any other roof in Aylis.

While engaged in the construction of his new home, Dr. Abasaliev didn't forget about relaxation. Every morning before dawn he went for a long walk to the Vang Church. There, in the spring that sputtered in the churchyard, he washed himself in the water clear as a tear, drank a glass of that water on an empty stomach, and filled up the big thermos he'd brought from Baku to use at home.

The whole Abasaliev family was highly respected in Aylis. And Dr. Abasaliev felt that respect with every step, a fact that, undoubtedly, made him very happy. The honor and respect shown him only increased the pleasure of those summer days spent in the village, strengthened the feeling of tranquility and freedom, and simplified and eased the relationship between the people of Aylis and their famous fellow villager.

Dr. Abasaliev was able to comfortably enter any home and converse with the owner. He familiarly scolded the women who didn't sweep their plots by the wicket gate or polluted the river bank with garbage. He supported the sick and helped the poor as much as he was able. And having spoken all of one time with Mirali *kishi*, who'd turned the church into his personal storehouse, he forever put to rest the war that the Armenian Aniko had waged for long years with that willful old man; on that same day, the old man not only cleared out the church but also thoroughly cleaned and washed everything there and with his own hands presented the keys to Aniko.

According to the stories of Dr. Abasaliev, at one time there had been a full twelve churches in Aylis. Sadai Sadygly knew where eight of them had been. The whereabouts of the remaining four ruins were unknown even to Dr. Abasaliev. Strictly speaking, it was incorrect even to call the eight churches "churches" because only the pitiful rubble of them now remained.

The most ancient of them was called Istazyn by the people of Aylis. Even now, it's almost impossible to convince anyone in Aylis that the correct name isn't Istazyn but Astvatsadun, which means "God's house" in Armenian, and that those ruins, of which only two walls and two basements have been preserved whole, were formerly Mecca and Medina for Armenians.

The surviving basements of that Armenian Mecca, standing a considerable distance from the village at the foot of the naked mountains where not one sapling grew; where there was not a scrap of shade; where on hot days the earth, stones, and gravel were all scorching hot like a tandoor oven and blazed with heat—those basements now served as shelter for herdsmen and livestock, and the destroyed walls stood as if just to remind people that everything on earth is transient, even if it's the home of God himself.

The other three churches (no one in Aylis remembered when they'd been destroyed) were the White Church (Ag Kilse), the Orphan Church (Etim Kilse), and the Church on the Square (Meidan Kilsesi). And the remaining churches—in Vuragyrd and Vang, the Stone Church, and Dop—although they'd been left without God and untended, all the same hadn't wholly lost their past grandeur. How those four churches were constructed—in such a way that behind each stood, in the literal sense of the word, a single mountain—the Muslim population of Aylis, naturally, never saw. However, there was no need to be Armenian or know the ABCs of history to see the harmonious unity that those churches created with the mountains standing behind them. Each church was the exact same color as the mountain next to it—as if it had been cut out whole from that mountain and placed there, where it was easy and comfortable for God to contemplate it. And each individual church, it seemed, was the natural child of that mountain at whose foot it had been built.

It was from Dr. Abasaliev that Sadai Sadygly learned that summer that the word Vang means "monastery" in Armenian. And it was precisely there, in the yard of the Vang Church, that Sadai saw his future father-in-law for the first time. There they exchanged their first words, began a conversation, and from then on they felt mutual goodwill and over time became friends.

That summer they wandered a great deal around Aylis (sometime as a twosome and sometimes with Azada accompanying them), making the rounds of its gardens, springs, and churches. They climbed up the mountains and hills. On other days, when the weather was a bit cooler, they crossed over the nearest mountain together and walked around the neighboring villages.

Often, having made arrangements in the evening, they met the next morning in an agreed-upon place. Sometimes Dr. Abasaliev himself even came to Sadai early in the morning and hurried him along: "Hurry up, young man, soon it'll be dawn." From then on Dr. Abasaliev called Sadai "young man."

For many years, every one of those summer days spent with Dr. Abasaliev in Aylis was imprinted in the memory of Sadai Sadygly as a real holiday, not only because of the interesting stories about Aylis but also for the pleasant, dry warmth of the weather and its fresh greenness, the taste of the water of the various springs, and the special affability of people.

One night they agreed to meet the next day and set out together on a far path—much further than Vuragyrd—to the summer pasture of the Aylis shepherds. Earlier, arriving in the village for the summer holidays, Sadai had dreamed about seeing those summer pastures just once. Sadai's childhood friend Jamal, who'd studied with him in the same class for seven years, had joined an elderly herdsman after the seventh grade and tended the collective farm herd in the mountains with him. From then on it was impossible to find Jamal in the village in summer. But it was difficult for Sadai to set out on his own to search for his friend in the mountains.

First they walked along the level road to the Vang Church. From there they descended to the river and entered the path leading upward. At that time there was no more water in the little mountain river of Aylis than in an ordinary spring. And it wasn't the kind of cold water that could quench a thirst as spring water could. But when they were growing especially hot on their long journey, that water came to their aid. All the same, they were only able to go as far as the weir. Understanding that without guides and horses or donkeys they wouldn't reach their goal, they somehow got back using the narrow paths built by herdsmen, and near noon they found themselves by the Vuragyrd Church, standing on the slope of the mountain—at the very highest point of Aylis.

Sadai had known that church from childhood. A great number of pigeons lived there, and for that reason its nickname among the people was the "Pigeon Bazaar." When they entered the church, the pigeons weren't there—they'd flown out among the gardens and fields, where there were grain and water in abundance. And because of that, a special atmosphere having nothing in common with the real world now reigned within the high, thick walls of the church—a special world of stillness and silence, a world without people and outside of time.

Even the air inside the church was somehow unearthly—not of this world, not of these parts. And the long, rectangular beams of light that had fallen from the narrow windows in the cupola didn't seem as if they were the light of Aylis—it seemed that light emanated from other far-off and unknown worlds. Even the light seeping through the crack that had formed not long before just below the cupola created the mystic feeling of another world inside the church.

Since childhood, Sadai had often dreamed of the stone steps leading from the channel of the river up towards the church, dreamed of the square paved with stones beneath those steps and of the narrow little street paved with those same stones running from there down towards the steep bank of the river. However, on that day when he and Dr. Abasaliev were returning from their unsuccessful journey, it seemed to Sadai that he was seeing the church; the little stone roads leading to it; its stone walls; and that strange, ancient, solitary street in Vuragyrd for the first time in his life. Something resembling a dream or a fairy tale was present in the landscape of the far-off Vuragyrd Quarter of Aylis that Sadai saw then—and Pessimist Gulu, well-known in Aylis, who was pacing by the gate of his house and loudly conversing with himself, only intensified the mystic mood that corresponded to that landscape in Sadai's soul.

Gulu hadn't changed in the least. When his fits began he always left his house, circled around in front of the gate, and for whole days passionately, loudly, and without ceasing conversed with himself from morning till night. He said that someone was pouring poison every day into the irrigation canal that ran into his yard. Gulu heaped the choicest abuse on the heads of those "saboteurs." He rained down terrible curses on the heads of the children who'd thrown stones in his yard or climbed onto his roof. From afar, he threatened the young people who for a long time had supposedly wanted passionately to seduce his hunchbacked wife and aged, sick daughters.

Dr. Abasaliev pulled a banknote from his pocket and thrust it into the pocket of Gulu. Gulu fell silent and looked at Dr. Abasaliev for a long time in surprise.

"Well, Gulu, don't you recognize me?" asked the doctor.

Pessimist Gulu thought for a little while, and then he suddenly clapped the doctor on the shoulder and said, "You're Zulfi, isn't that so? And I recognized your companion immediately. Even when he was a little boy, he hung around here every day, doing nothing." Gulu shook the doctor firmly by the shoulder. "Listen, Zulfi, how'd you end up here?"

"Ah, well, I came to see how you're getting along with your jinns," answered Dr. Abasaliev, winking discreetly at Sadai. "Well, Pessimist, what are they whispering to you this time? Do they come only at night, or do they torment you during the day, too?"

"That's what you came to say to me?!" said the outraged Gulu. "And you call yourself a doctor."

"So, then, you're finished with jinns? And did you plant anything in your yard this year?"

"Of course I planted something, why wouldn't I?!" Pessimist Gulu announced loudly, but he immediately changed the subject. "But do those scoundrels allow anything to be harvested from what's sown?"

"But you say the jinns have left you alone."

"Of course they leave me alone! Everyone who lives here is a hundred times more terrible than jinns." Pessimist Gulu kicked open the gate. "Just look for yourself. See, those scoundrels poured poison in my water—and all my trees started to wither."

Sadai looked into the yard; the trees were mainly apricot trees, with a few apple, pear, hazelnut, and peach trees. A goat whose udder hung down below her knees was tied to a cherry tree. A few hens with chicks scratched between the branches of a barberry growing by the wall. Nothing had been planted in the yard. But not one of the trees looked like it had withered.

"You know he's an old nut case, young man," Dr. Abasaliev said after they walked away from Gulu's gate. Heading down the little paved street and not taking his eyes off the surrounding houses, he began to tell Sadai an entirely unexpected, terrible, and strange story.

"I'll tell you something, young man, only I'm afraid you'll think I'm a nut case, too. Here in Aylis there really are a lot of jinns. Now, by jinns, I mean ghosts. Do you know in whose home Gulu lives? At one time an Armenian, a cross-eyed stonemason by the name of Minas, lived there. And his ancestors were stonemasons from ancient times. The stones of many of the churches are the work of Minas' ancestors. And Minas worked with stone from the day he was born; he produced gravestones, mortars, millstones, and many other things. . . The grandfather of that nut case Gulu, Abdulla, was exactly the sort of loafer and nitwit his grandson is. He worked as a porter in the bazaar, carried water from the stream to the tearoom, and earned a few pitiful coins with which he made do. And what do you know, when Adif Bey ordered the extermination of the Armenians in Aylis, that jackal Abdulla suddenly plucked up his courage. He ran home, snatched up an ax, and burst into Minas' house. Minas was quietly sitting and working a stone. That scoundrel Abdulla attacked him with the ax and chopped off his head, and then he spared neither the poor man's wife nor children. If you would be so good, please explain to me how that Gulu can now live tranquilly in Minas' house? He can't, I swear to God! The ghost of the tormented Minas will never give him peace. God is not so forgetful as to forgive such monstrous villany."

Evidently, the mystic landscape of Vuragyrd strongly affected Dr. Abasaliev then, too. He stopped often, surveying the river stones polished over a thousand years with which the road beneath their feet was paved. With unceasing surprise he looked at the ruined and falling-down old houses, unable to tear his eyes from the yards and trees. And perhaps it was on exactly that day after the conversation with Pessimist Gulu that, with the genuine passion of a psychologist, he decided to research and substantiate the vexing ideas that suddenly took up residence in his own consciousness.

"In every Aylis family," he began irritably, in a somewhat-odd voice, "that seized an Armenian home, there are mentally ill people; I say that to you as a doctor. Did you ever once see peace in any of those homes? Let's list all the homes below Vuragyrd if you doubt it. We'll start with the home of Myryg Muzaffar standing next to the Stone Church. Neither he himself nor his wife was distinguished by mental deviations. Because the houses in which they were born and grew up weren't seized at the time of the pogroms. But look at their children: all mentally ill. Moreover, with a classic form of schizophrenia. In my time at the hospital, I treated two of Muzaffar's daughters. And treated them properly. Now you can meet those girls on the street, at the spring. They have the look of sick sheep. They don't say hello to anyone, don't talk with anyone. Because it's an incurable illness.

"I think it's not even an illness but a punishment. Punishment sent by God to man for his unforgivable conduct. . . A little below Myryg Muzaffar stands the house of Wild Man Gulam. You see the state his grandson is in? He climbs on the fence and throws stones at passersby. Now, look at what's happening in the other houses seized at the time of the pogroms. Gafil, the son of the old woman Beyaz, is outwardly a normal person. But he's also cuckoo. The other day he stopped me in the street and talked for a good hour about how Mohammed flew up Mount Sinai on a black horse for a meeting with Allah.

"Well, that's enough, we'll leave the mentally ill. Not one person in Aylis who at that time tried to improve his own life through violence against the Armenians knows peace to this day. You yourself hear how the two sons of Gazanfar who seized the house from *Mugdisi* Alekhsan bawl and curse every night. Those brothers are prepared to gnaw one another's throats. That's how children bear the punishment for a sin committed by parents. The ghosts of those we've tormented won't give us peace. Look at Mamedaga the butcher, who hacked the daughter of Mkrtych the priest to death in the street with his dagger. I didn't see him in his old age. But those who traveled to Baku said he kicked the bucket like a dog. First he went completely blind, then he suffered a stroke—his mouth was twisted up towards his ears. Besides, the scoundrel suffered dreadfully from constipation. When he strained in the bathroom, his moans carried all the way to Zangezur. Even today, people are ready to spit on his grave. In a word, young man, I no longer believe that sometime better times will arrive here. And I see that the people of Aylis don't believe it themselves."

Moving a little further from Gulu's house, Dr. Abasaliev opened the first wicket gate he came to and went into the yard.

Old Nubar, the mistress of the house, sat on the veranda sorting wool and talking loudly to herself. Seeing guests, she rejoiced with all her soul.

"Come in, come in," she greeted them. "Welcome! How is it that you suddenly remembered about me, Mr. Doctor? They say you've been here a month already, and I'm just seeing you for the first time."

"And whose fault is that? Do you ever leave your home so people can see you?" Dr. Abasaliev looked around the yard. "Thank God, you have a beautiful yard. And an abundance of water, it seems."

"May the Lord gladden you with all things in abundance, Zulfi *gardash*. So long as I have the strength, I'll look after my household. And to our good fortune, this year there's enough water. Much better than in previous years. And now I'll light the samovar and make you tea."

"Not to worry, we're leaving now. I just dropped in for a minute to find out how you're doing. You're all by yourself, still?"

"By myself, Mr. Doctor, by myself," old Nubar uttered mournfully. "I lost one of my daughters when she was just a girl. She fell in love with some rascal and stupidly doused herself in kerosene and burned to death. I married off two girls who went away. And my son left and married a Russian, so he doesn't show his face here anymore."

"And do you remember the Armenian who lived in this house?"

Old Nubar was surprised.

"That was Arakel, you yourself know better than I do. And it's as if it happened just yesterday—his wife Eskhi threw herself off the cliff. How beautiful she was! Do you remember how she sang at weddings? At both their Armenian weddings and our Muslim ones. . . A curse on that Adif Bey! When his army came into Aylis, poor Eskhi lost her mind. You remember it—every day just as the sun set, she was already up on Khyshkeshen Mountain, where she climbed on the cliff and wept while she loudly sang:

> *Adif Bey, don't slay us, don't slay us,*
> *We're the flowers of Aylis, have mercy, spare us."*

"And who killed Arakel in this house?" Dr. Abasaliev asked uncertainly.

"But you know Arakel wasn't killed at home, Mr. Doctor!" old Nubar answered, astonished. "The son of the snake catcher Abdulali killed Arakel on his plot of land. I know what you're getting at, but no one's blood was spilled in this house."

The doctor thought seriously.

"That may be," he said, "Yes, perhaps I was mistaken. And to whom were you talking when we entered the yard?"

"Well, who's left for me to talk to?" Tears appeared in old Nubar's eyes. "I just talk to myself."

Old Nubar's tears clearly moved the doctor.

"And do you believe in ghosts, Nubar?" he asked in a shaken voice.

"I believe in them, Mr. Doctor, exactly as I believe in Allah and the Prophet! You know it was those ghosts who led us to such a life, Zulfi, may your grief pass on to me. Do you remember that

Iranian from Maragheh? Do you remember what he said on his last visit—long before the slaughter of the Armenians—that Maragheh merchant who often came through here selling all kinds of spices, persimmons, chewing gum, ginger, and cinnamon? 'Leave this place before it's too late,' he said, 'A person can't live in a place where there are so many cemeteries without knowing woe.'" Old Nubar smiled through her tears and suddenly sighed so painfully and deeply that a long wheeze burst from her ancient chest. "But honestly, Zulfi *gardash*, even if they lived a thousand years, the Muslims of Aylis would never have done evil to their longtime neighbors. It was after the command of that cursed Adif Bey that greed enveloped our people. If your father *Hajji* Hasan had been here then, perhaps people would have felt ashamed before him, and they wouldn't have robbed the Armenians. Five or six villains who'd long hankered after Armenian property stained their hands with blood because of their greed."

Dr. Abasaliev heard the story of old Nubar with great attention, as if it were news to him. Although only a few days earlier he'd told Sadai that story himself, moveover, with almost the same details. Nubar was part of the older generation of inhabitants of Aylis. However, at the time there were still more than a few middle-aged people in Aylis who'd seen the unprecedented slaughter of the Armenians of Aylis with their own eyes.

Everyone told of that slaughter in their own way, coming from their own understanding of man and humanity. Nevertheless, none of the witnesses of those events hid what they'd seen. The exact same facts were reliably present in the stories of different people. In terms of how everything began and ended, the opinions of people fully agreed.

This is what happened. So that the Armenian population of Aylis wouldn't suspect anything beforehand, thirty to forty Turkish horsemen of Adif Bey had been riding around all the houses—both Armenian and Muslim—since early morning and announcing that on that day a truce would be declared, and therefore everyone needed to gather immediately in the yard of a certain Armenian. After that, as people assembled in the appointed place, the Turkish soldiers divided Muslims from Armenians and stood them in rows on opposite sides of the yard. Suddenly, a loud command rang out from somewhere: "Fire!" The Turkish soldiers surrounding the yard on all sides rained down a hail of bullets on the Armenians. Many perished immediately. Those who survived had their throats cut with daggers or were stabbed to death by bayonets, to the very last person. Digging a ditch, they buried those they could bury right there in the yard and the garden. They threw those for whom there wasn't space in the yard and garden into the stables and cellars of the nearest homes and burned them. The Muslim women who on that day didn't even dare leave their homes later described events this way: "The water in all the irrigation canals was red with blood for an entire week." And this: "Adif Bey had a horse that was black like a crow. Adif sat on him by the gates of the house. Shouting 'Fire!' he lashed his horse with his crop and galloped off. And immediately the rain of bullets began to flow; it seemed as if the sky had fallen, ash rained down from above. A cry went up such as no one had heard since the creation of the world. All the dogs in the yards began barking all at once. All the crows in the trees began cawing. The frightened magpies and pigeons disappeared instantly from the village; they flew off to hide beyond the mountains. It seemed as if hell had opened up, as if the sun were just about to crash down to earth!'"

Not once had Sadai Sadygly ever heard anyone remember that slaughter in Aylis without horror and sympathy. And all Sadai's knowledge of his hometown was closely connected with those tragic events.

Only after his acquaintance with Dr. Abasaliev did the artist in full measure begin to understand the true worth of that small geographic expanse called Aylis that—thanks, perhaps, to its being well built, and to the cleanliness and neatness of its streets that staggered the imagination—had once been nicknamed "Little Paris" or "Little Istanbul." Only then did he grasp the significance of the unparalleled culture created there through the work and intelligence of people who believed deeply in God. Dr. Abasaliev, according to his own words, was not only an "Aylis fanatic"; he was its historian and psychologist and even a sort of philosopher. Only from Dr. Abasaliev did Sadai Sadygly learn that the famous monk Mesrop Mashtots had invented the Armenian alphabet right there in Aylis and that the well-known writer Raffi had taught at the local school in his time. "Aylis, young man, that's divine perfection!" Dr. Abasaliev exclaimed to Sadai many times. "And for what we did to it, we'll be called to answer before God on Judgment Day."

According to Dr. Abasaliev, a certain Armenian girl who'd been saved from the slaughter in 1919 cultivated a new flower in France that she called Agulis, that is, Aylis. And the artist Gayane Khachaturian, who from age nine or ten drew just the Aylis churches for the rest of her life, lived in Tbilisi. In sum, from the stories of Dr. Abasaliev it turned out that Aylis was indeed one of the thousand-and-one names of God. And possibly his love for Aylis had absolutely no connection to Armenians or to Muslims. More likely, it was one more distinctive and truly noble manifestation of man's faithfulness to Truth.

"That Nubar was extremely intelligent from childhood. At that time she still went to Mirza Vahab, who'd studied in Istanbul, to learn to read and write." Dr. Abasaliev pronounced those words when they'd already walked far away from Nubar's house. It seems he was upset by their visit to her—shaken either by her utter sincerity or for some other reason. And if they hadn't met Zohra *arvad* a little later, then probably he would have returned home in a bad mood.

Having flung open one half of the gate, apparently so as to see people passing in the street, Zohra *arvad* had settled herself comfortably on the steps leading to the veranda and was drinking steaming tea. The entire yard, from the wicket gate to those same steps up to the veranda, was swept clean and sprinkled with water. A narrow little stream of water flowed through the whole yard along the long pathway planted with various flowers. Zohra *arvad*'s yard pleased the eye in every sense of the word. Shapely lemon trees grown in special large pots—so they could be carried indoors during winter— stood near the stream in front of the veranda, giving the yard a particular charm.

Those potted lemon trees had formerly belonged to Aikanush; Sadai had known them long and well. But the strangest thing was that even Dr. Abasiliev recognized Aikanush's lemons at first glance.

"Listen, why did you drag Aikanush's lemons here?" he'd asked from the wicket gate, not yet entering the yard.

"What? You see a lemon, and already your mouth is watering? And again you fail to notice such a beauty as I am?"

"And what's left of your beauty? All unraveled, eh, Zohra, my soul!"

Between them, evidently, lay a long, friendly relationship that allowed them to joke with one another.

"And what's with you? Here you are—all of you, like a piece of candy." Zohra *arvad* brought three old stools from the veranda and set them under the lemons near the little stream. "Come in, sit down. Now I'll give you some excellent tea—tea from India-land. Where are you coming from in all this heat?" Zohra *arvad* brought two glasses, stood them on one of the stools, picked a ripe lemon from the branch and, slicing it, asked, "And why didn't you bring your wife?"

"She didn't want to come." Dr. Abasaliev poured tea into the saucer and, blowing on it, sipped it with pleasure. "Something's not right with her heart, Zohra. She's afraid to travel very far."

"And they say your daughter's going to be a dentist? So be it, God willing. What use do I have for a doctor like you? Maybe your daughter can give me new teeth," said Zohra *arvad*, stroking her toothless gums.

Dr. Abasaliev's mood gradually improved.

"And what did you do with the unfortunate Khankishi? You dispatched him to the other world, did you?"

"If only an unlucky snake would bite that Khankishi, Zulfi! Did that son of a bitch really live with me? Three years he had his way with me, lived it up day and night. And then ran away from me like a tomcat on the prowl. You see, he had no need of a barren wife. After me, that jackal got married two more times, but he remained childless like before. And he finally figured out that it wasn't me but his seed that was barren." Zohra *arvad* gently stroked Dr. Abasaliev's back. "But what was I to do, you didn't marry me, you went off, found yourself a city girl."

And here Dr. Abasaliev's well-known, ordinarily sharp wit failed him. He suddenly turned deep red and, so as to somehow get out of the situation, quickly changed the subject.

"So your greatest girlfriend really deserted you? Somehow these lemons are painfully familiar to me."

"Of course they're her lemons. Who else in the village had such lemons as Aikanush?" said Zohra *arvad*, pouring tea into the glasses. "Yes, Mr. Doctor, Aikanush moved away. Last fall she collected her things and moved to Yerevan to her son Zhora. If it had been up to her, I doubt she'd have moved there. Zhora absolutely insisted. If you'd seen how she was when she was leaving! She simply couldn't part with her house, her yard. She circled around her trees like a crazy woman. She kissed and embraced even the rotten beams on her veranda. And just before she left, she came here, stood and wept in front of these lemons as if she weren't leaving lemons here but seven of her own children. And since then I've looked after her house. This year the lemons ripened well—I collected a whole big bucket and sent them to her. Our people carry goods to Yerevan from here year-round; I asked them, and they took the lemons." Zohra *arvad* picked two lemons, bright yellow among the green leaves, and laid them on the stool. "Here's one for each of you. Drink tea at home. I left three or four on each tree for just such dear guests as you."

Relaxing after tea, Dr. Abasaliev sat and smiled sadly, looking at the lemons. And then he asked, simply to keep up the conversation, "And Aikanush hasn't invited you to Yerevan?"

"She has invited me. She's asked a number of times through our Aylis people working in the Yerevan bazaar: 'Please tell my sister that she should come, stay here with me for ten or fifteen days.'" Zohra *arvad* laughed and winked at the doctor. "Well, what do you say? Should I go, so that in my old age I can lose what little is left of being Muslim there, in an Armenian home?"

"As if this home of yours isn't Armenian!"

"Look at this old rogue!" exclaimed Zohra *arvad*, addressing Sadai. "And from where would Mr. Doctor get the brains to treat crazy people?" Then, half-laughing, half-serious, she shook her finger at the doctor. "My father Meshdali bought this house from Uncle Arutiun-Samvel for fifteen gold *tomans*. As if you didn't know!"

"I know. I didn't mean it that way."

Zohra *arvad* fell silent, considering something to herself, then seriously and anxiously whispered, "I'm not offended, even if you speak ill of my father. Only, for the love of God, Zulfi, don't ever mention the name of the executioner Mamedaga. His foul spawn is worse than the man himself. I mean that Jinn-Eye Shaban, Zulfi. They say he even did you a dirty trick. Don't get involved with them, you can't expect anything good from that tribe."

"And how did you find out about that?" he asked with infinite surprise, fidgeting noticeably.

"As if anything could be concealed in this village. The women were gossiping about it the other day at the spring. They say he dug up an old skull somewhere and threw it across the fence into your yard, and that he stuck a note into the skull: 'Here I am, Mkrtych the priest, cousin of the Armenian spy Zulfi Abasaliev.'"

Seeing that the doctor was upset, Zohra *arvad* fell silent.

Sadai was hearing the story of the skull for the first time, although he'd long known that it was hardly possible to find a person more despicable and spiteful than Jinn-Eye Shaban, son of the butcher Mamedaga who'd killed the daughter of the priest Mkrtych. That Jinn-Eye Shaban, five or six years older than Sadai, was the very same Shaban who since the age of ten or eleven had carried a butcher knife in his pocket and a hunting rifle over his shoulder. It was with that same rifle that Shaban once shot a tiny, black, and beautiful fox cub on the fence of the Stone Church, a cub that for some unknown reason had turned up that spring in Aylis. And although at the time Sadai had been four or five, he never forgot that event and many times leapt up at night from the sound of that fateful shot. Rain and snow had long since washed the blood of the dead cub from the fence; however, in Sadai's mind a scarlet spot of blood remained on the wall of the fence forever.

That same hellraiser Shaban was probably spreading rumors about the skull thrown over the fence and the words written on the note around Aylis now. However, Dr. Abasaliev never again mentioned the foul escapade of Mamedaga's spawn.

Aikanush, the former mistress of the lemon trees, was one of two Armenian women whom Sadai had often seen and known more or less well in childhood. In Aylis there were also a few more Armenian women. However, they didn't differ at all from the Azerbaijani women and for that reason weren't preserved in Sadai's childhood memories.

The first summer when Sadai came home for summer break after studying in Baku, Aikanush was still living in Aylis. She was already stooped from old age and eternally working the earth, but she still had the ability to manage her household. With her own hands she hoed the earth in the little yard right by the river, growing her own beans, potatoes, cucumbers, tomatoes, and greens there. She herself tended her lemon trees, the fame of which spread throughout Aylis. She even sent pears, peaches, dried fruit, and *sujug*—fruit sausage stuffed with nuts—to her son Zhora in Yerevan. On Armenian holy days she walked around the Vang Church, prayed for hours, and made the sign of the cross over herself. Tired out from work, she sat by her gates and conversed with her closest neighbor and longtime friend, Zohra *arvad*.

Aikanush's house stood a good distance from the Vang Church in a low-lying area on the bank of the river closer to the Muslim part of the village. In spite of that, the church became a second home for old Aikanush. Coming through the high, strong gates that no cannon had ever breached, each time she saw the church it was as if she'd lost her reason. Like a crazy person, she began making circles around the church. Then she kissed its stone walls almost stone by stone, making the sign of the cross over herself. Finally old Aikanush went up to the doors and stopped before them. There she crossed herself several times before the stone image of the woman holding a baby whom the Aylis Muslims nicknamed "Turbaned Woman with a Babe in Arms." With that, she ended her pilgrimage, which looked like an amusing performance when seen from a distance.

As a child Sadai saw Aikanush's son Zhora—who lived in Yerevan—several times in Aylis. And when Zhora's daughter Lyusik came from Yerevan to Aylis, Sadai was already eleven or twelve and was one of three inseparable schoolmate-friends: Sary (Light-Haired) Sadai, Bomb Babash, and Jambul Jamal.

They were always together when they went to collect stray spike-lets of grain from the field after the grain harvest. Together they clambered over the mountains and cliffs in search of partridge eggs. And when there was no school, no work on the threshing floor, and they were tired of playing *babki* in the street, they started in on the churches. Using river stones heavy from moisture, they tried to break off a nose or ear of the marble statues in the yard of the Stone Church and smash the stone crosses carved on the Vang walls. They climbed onto the high Vuragyrd roof and loudly cat-called the vil-lage from above. They ran roughshod over the peas, beans, and corn planted by Mirali *kishi* in the yard of the Vang Church and the bright flowers planted by Anykh-Aniko. Or else they inscribed their names on the walls of the church with the sharp-edged stones found at the bottom of the river, which they always carried in their pockets: Sary Sadai! Bomb Babash! Jambul Jamal!

Light-colored hair had been passed to "Sary" Sadai as the legacy of his ancestors—their family members were all blonds. Babash had received the nickname "Bomb" because of his proud disposition, endless agility, and his iron health and strength. The nickname that Jamal bore, "Jambul," had a special and sad history.

They belonged to the prewar generation, having been born a couple of years before the start of the war that took away their fathers. However, three or four years after the end of the war, news suddenly arrived that Jamal's father Bony Safi was alive. His wife Dilruba received a letter from Safi in which he simply announced that he hadn't perished in the war, that he was alive and healthy and lived now in a land called Kazakhstan in the city of Jambul. He wrote that he'd married again and that his new wife had given birth to a son. He announced that he'd never come back to Aylis, but if his son Jamal wanted, he could come join him in the city of Jambul.

After that ill-starred letter, the wailing of Jamal's grandmother Azra brought the whole village to their feet in the dead of night: her daughter Dilruba had poured a can of kerosene over her head and tried to burn herself to death.

After that, Jamal's mother simply couldn't right herself. She didn't eat or drink, didn't sleep at night, stopped doing the simplest tasks, and completely abandoned the house. Finally losing possession of her wits, she tramped around the mountains at night like a wild animal; she was searching for her husband to punish him, but she didn't know the road to Jambul. They found the body of Jamal's mother at the edge of the highway some twenty to twenty-five miles from Aylis. That's how that idiotic nickname stuck to Jamal—"Jambul."

Living in Baku, Sadai remembered Jamal almost every day. And each time he remembered Jamal, he also remembered the Vang Church: its yard, the tall and shapely cherry tree, and old Aikanush with a shawl invariably hanging down her back. Sleeves rolled up above her elbows, almost crying from stupefaction, she was diligently washing Jamal's lice-ridden head.

That morning the three of them had climbed the tall cherry tree in the churchyard. That year the weather had already been very hot for a long time, but all the same Jamal hadn't taken off the dirty cloth cap for which he'd been made to sit all winter at the last desk in class. Right up until the summer holidays, their faculty advisor Myleila *muallima* had dedicated the majority of the lessons to discussing that cap. As if she didn't know that after Grandmother Azra had gone blind during the winter, no one had washed Jamal's hair once, and Jamal himself, depressed by the sudden death of his mother, hadn't found the strength to wash even once.

It turns out that old Aikanush knew this better than any of the others. Moreover, somehow old Aikanush found out that on that morning Jambul Jamal was going to be there in the churchyard. While the boys sat in the tree, she started a fire right under the cherry tree; heated water in a large copper pot; and brought soap, a towel, a pitcher, and some sort of mud-like mass—black, like tar, with which she planned to grease Jamal's head afterwards—in a pint-sized jar from home.

Hardly had old Aikanush removed the cap from Jamal's head than Babash vomited up the cherries they'd been stuffing into their stomachs. Sadai simply closed his eyes and turned away. Aikanush shrieked "*Vai!*" as if she'd been stung and grabbed her head with both hands. There were as many lice on Jamal's head as ants in an anthill.

Old Aikanush sat Jamal by the fire on a flat river rock. Sadai filled the pitcher with warm water and poured it on Jamal's head, and Aikanush rubbed that lice-ridden head with soap, combing with her fingernails until it bled. Then she again soaped and washed it, saying in a quiet, mournful voice, "My child. Poor boy. Poor orphan!"

And lying unconscious now on a bed in the Baku hospital, Sadai Sadygly heard that voice so clearly, so close by, that even if old Aikanush had turned out to be right next to him in the room, that mournful voice wouldn't have sounded so distinctly.

And Sadai Sadygly heard equally clearly the shouts of the women hurrying from their homes to the churchyard when old Aikanush, having already washed and smeared Jamal's head with medicine, bandaged his head with gauze.

"We call ourselves Muslims and yet didn't have enough sense to wash the boy's head."

"Look, she washed it, so what if she's not Muslim. You know Aikanush didn't fall from the sky! She's also from our village."

"May God be with you in times of trouble, Aikanush *baji*! You've always been known by your kindness towards us Muslims."

"Who wouldn't wash the head of an orphan? How were we to know that the poor boy had lice?"

"What, you didn't see that he never took the cap off his head? If he didn't have lice, would he have gone around in a cap in this heat?"

"May Allah protect your only son in Yerevan, Aikanush. You're the most merciful of our Aylis women."

"You, Aikanush, love Allah, so what if you're Armenian!"

After washing her hands thoroughly with soap and rubbing the small of her back draped with the shawl, Aikanush could barely manage to straighten up. One by one the women dispersed. And as soon as their voices ceased, Aikanush stretched out her hands and moved towards the church with such fervor that it seemed that small, frail woman would now clasp that whole, huge stone thing to her breast like a baby.

When old Aikanush made the sign of the cross before the "Tubaned Woman," Jamal, white gauze on his head, sat silently by the wall in front of the entrance to the church. And Lyusik, who up until now had squeezed herself into a corner of the gate, observing with fear and horror how her grandmother washed Jamal's head, now stood up, leaning against the trunk of the cherry tree and, it seemed, crying quietly. And tears also shone in Jamal's eyes. He gazed with amazement on the world, as if he were seeing it for the first time. Babash stood next to him, hanging his head low; he was embarrassed that he hadn't been able to control himself just now and thrown up so shamefully.

And Aikanush, as usual, stood by the church entrance and prayed furiously. What kind of miracle took place on earth that day so that Sadai, who until that moment hadn't understood a single word of Armenian, suddenly began to understand every word that Aikanush was whispering very quietly, almost to herself? Is it possible he dreamed it? Or did that mystic, spiritual-heavenly gift of the great Creator descend on Sadai—the Creator who at least once in life shows a miracle to every one of his creations whom he named people? And who knows, did that "Turbaned Woman" gazing forever on the world with dead stone eyes really just forget that she was carved of stone to suddenly, gently, smile at Sadai? And the baby she held in her arms suddenly came to life, began to turn his neck, to move his arms and legs. With his own eyes, Sadai saw how the infant, opening his eyes wide, winked happily at someone. And—why is it,

O Creator—why were the eyes of the infant at the same time the eyes of Jamal? Let's say all this was a hallucination—a dream or a vision—but from where, then, did that voice sound, the voice of Lame Chimnaz, the deformed daughter of Jinni Sakina, who lived next to the church?

"Look, people! Sadai Sadygly is crossing himself like an Armenian!"

And that disgusting "specimen of folklore" that the idiot Chimnaz sang loudly after that in her disgusting voice?

> *The Armenian, hey, the Armenian*
> *In the mountains threshes grain.*
> *He's got a son and a daughter,*
> *Up his ass is a buffalo horn.*[2]

And also that unearthly light?!

How did it happen that on the day when Sadai suddenly understood the prayer of old Aikanush and for the first time in his life unconsciously crossed himself, the yellow-rose light of the eyes of the Almighty—which usually shone gently on the church cupola and the top of the mountain alone—spilled over everywhere? Never again did Sadai Sadygly see the earth so lit up with unimaginably bright light, but he never stopped believing that in Aylis there exists some other light that belongs only to Aylis. Sadai was deeply convinced that it really must be so—you see, in both length and breadth Upper Aylis probably encompassed no more than three or four miles. And if the people who at some time raised twelve churches on that tiny scrap of earth and created a heavenly corner near each of them had *not* left just a little of their light after themselves, then for what reason does a person need God?

And had anyone besides Sadai seen how that yellow-rose radiance spilled over all of Aylis that day? And why hadn't he dared to ask anyone about it on that same day, there in the churchyard? Now, in Baku there was only Babash to ask about it. But how? Which Babash? To ask today's Babash Ziyadov about that day and that radiance would be as laughable as asking the head of the housing office the address of the Lord God.

That summer Bomb Babash, beginning to act like Majnun, had circled continuously around Lyusik, Aikanush's granddaughter from Yerevan, trying out every kind of pitiful trick. First he climbed up to the top of the tallest trees, crowing like a rooster and cawing like a crow; then, hiding in the bushes, he emitted the cries of a partridge. He bleated like a ram and howled like a wolf. Several times a day he walked on his hands with his feet in the air, making a circle around the church. "*Iski sarumis! Iski sarumis!*" he yelled, first from behind the fence, then from the roof of the church, mistakenly thinking he was declaring his love to Lyusik in Armenian.

However, thin and dark like her grandma, Lyusik patiently bore all these tricks; she didn't pay any attention to Babash, didn't notice him at all. Not seeing anything or anyone around her, Lyusik busied herself whole days in the churchyard with her brushes and paints.

Naturally, old Aikanush, who was responsible for every day her twelve-year-old granddaughter spent in the village, looked in at the church once a day without fail, bringing her tea in a thermos and hot lunch in a pan. But Lyusik never told her about Babash's escapades. Over time Aikanush herself somehow found out about his pranks and went to the Ziyadov house and complained to Babash's grandfather about his grandson's mischief. After that, Babash seemed to stay away from Lyusik. However, it turned out that the main scandal was yet to come.

It happened during those same summer holidays. One day a rumor went around the village that someone had climbed into Aikanush's yard during the night and picked a single lemon from each of her trees. Of course, it wasn't a serious theft, someone had simply wanted to offend the person to whom the lemons belonged. Aikanush, who suspected Babash more than anyone, all the same didn't complain to anyone. But two days later someone again climbed into Aikanush's yard at night and this time pulled down Lyusik's underwear, which had been hanging on the clothesline. The next morning was the last of their many years of unbreakable friendship and perhaps the end of all their light-filled, sunny childhood.

That morning, on the small square in front of the mosque where the Aylis kids usually played, even Sadai himself didn't understand how he felled Babash—considered the strongest of the boys—and was extremely surprised that Babash collapsed to the ground at his blow. Then he snatched the underwear Babash had been brandishing from his hands, displayed it to the kids, and yelled with all his might:

"This isn't Lyusik's, it belongs to Babash's sister, Rasima! So, who wants Rasima's underwear? I'm selling, come and get it!"

After that, although they sat in the same class for a year or a year and a half, they didn't speak to one another, not even in greeting. Later they sort of made up. However, the coolness between them always remained. Even after they'd moved to Baku to study, they didn't once make the attempt to find one another. Later Sadai found out that Babash, while still a student, had found work in the central committee of the Komsomol and was successfully making a career. And each time he heard about Babash's appointment to the next, more important post up the ladder, Sadai involuntarily remembered the church, Lyusik, Aikanush's lemons, the square in front of the mosque, and Babash brandishing Lyusik's underwear.

The next day Aikanush settled her granddaughter on the train at the Ordubad station and sent her back to Yerevan. After that, Lyusik didn't come to Aylis once.

The second prominent and colorful Armenian woman in Aylis was Aniko, whom everyone called Anykh. She was a courageous woman, proud and determined. She was able to do everything, knew everything, and could give useful advice to forest beekeepers about beekeeping and to silk worm breeders about the cultivation of silk worms. She treated the ailing and the sick in the village without having a medical education; only Allah knows how there was so much passion and strength in that woman! Aniko was a witness to how, on that black fall day in 1919, Turkish soldiers—after exterminating people with bullets and hacking them to pieces with sabers—drowned everyone great and small in a lake of blood. Among the dead were her parents, brothers, and sisters. All Aylis knew the ten-year-old Aniko had hidden then in a tandoor oven and survived only by accident; she stayed there three or four days without food or drink until Mirza Vahab's mother Zahra *arvad* discovered her. Mirza Vahab, who'd been educated in Istanbul and according to Dr. Abasaliev was considered the most learned Muslim in Aylis, was then about thirty years old. He hid Aniko in his house, raised her, and—of course forcibly—made her his wife. If not the greatest miracle in the world, what, then, should one consider the care and tenderness Aniko showed her husband, who was twenty years older than she was? She always spoke of him with pride and boasted of his learning, knowledge, and nobility. Aniko gave Mirza Vahab two sons and a daughter; the name of her husband was always on her lips.

Here, there, and everywhere she talked loudly about the fact that she'd converted to the Muslim faith.

And just as passionately, not afraid of anyone, about the fact that a time would certainly come when Armenians would return to Aylis, and it would again become a heavenly place.

During the days of mourning for the imams, the self-described Muslim Aniko didn't forget to sit in someone's home along with other women in the chador, loudly bewailing the cruelly murdered grandsons of the Prophet Mohammed; nevertheless, early almost every morning she went to the Vang Church. There she swept the churchyard, tended the beautiful, bright flowers she herself had sowed, and didn't let slip a chance to fearlessly rain down a stream of abuse on the head of all the ancestors of Mirali *kishi* who, turning the church into his personal storehouse, had hung locks on all the doors.

And Aniko's home itself on all sides resembled a celebratory exhibition of never-fading flowers, one that could be found nowhere else in Aylis. Mirza Vahab had settled in that house after the Armenian slaughter in 1919. They even said that the house, one of the most beautiful in Aylis, had personally been given to Mirza Vahab (who'd received his education in Istanbul) by Adif Bey, the leader of the Turks. How could one not believe, after that, that it was only miracle guiding all of Aniko's actions if, precisely in the location where the most bloody massacre caused by Adif Bey had taken place, she'd turned the yard into a veritable flower bed? Of course Aniko must have known. Perhaps, cultivating her flowers, she pursued a fixed goal—perhaps she wanted to immortalize the memory of each of her murdered fellow-tribesmen. To show that after every murdered Armenian a flower remained on the earth. And that she wanted every single Muslim in Aylis to understand that. It's possible that the blood once spilled in that yard still seethed in Aniko's memory and that the only way to soothe the blood-soaked memory was for her to adorn her yard and all the pathways of the Vang Church with flowers.

Aniko remained in Sadai's memory not only as a fine person and woman but also as a particular kind of voice, happy and ringing. A voice that encompassed in itself all of Aylis—with its homes, churches, mountains, roads, trees, streams, and springs—and a ringing herald of approaching morning. Because Aniko always woke at dawn and loudly sang on her high veranda, as if she wanted to announce to all the Muslims of Aylis that an Armenian voice still lived and sounded in Aylis.

In contrast to Aikanush, she always went to the Vang Church noisily, walking along the old coach road in the mountain and talking loudly. She recalled Eskhi, who'd thrown herself from the cliff, and cursed Adif Bey for all to hear, and from a distance began scolding Mirali *kishi*, who'd turned the most beautiful Aylis church into his own pathetic storeroom. The voice of Aniko, who never forgot to mention she'd converted to Islam and become the wife of such a noble and learned man as Mirza Vahab, it seemed, had nothing in common with the voice of the little Armenian orphan girl saved by a miracle from a Turkish bayonet. This, beyond all doubt, was the voice of the true mistress of Aylis, reaching from the depths of time. In a word, it was the morning voice of Aylis!

Living in Baku, Sadai Sadygly often heard it in his Aylis dreams, and many Baku mornings began for the artist with that exact same voice.

At the very same time when the dirty, corrupt mug of the old world, like an old whore, was just beginning to show signs of the fiendishly unavoidable clash of Muslim and Armenian on itself, Sadai Sadygly dreamed of a strange church. The strange thing was that it didn't look like any of the Aylis churches. And at the same time, there was something of each of them in its frightening, mystical look.

In the dream it was impossible to tell the time of year. It was early morning in Aylis: dawn had just commenced, the village was dragging itself with difficulty out of the dark of night. In the mountains, on the shady side, snow still lay in little islands. Above them were rare, fleecy white clouds. And still there was that cosmic, mystical light, both alien and to the highest degree native, familiar!

The high, white walls of the church that appeared to Sadai in the dream had cracked from the inside, and that light could be seen filtering into the church through the cracks that had formed.

A sound resembling the hum of a swarm of bees streamed without stopping, a sound bringing horror with it, pouring directly into the church as if from some entirely different world and from there—through the cracked walls—hurrying with diabolical passion to spread the terrible news it brought around the world.

And from that time that strange, unearthly sound followed Sadai without stopping. From the radio—from the television screen—from the revolutionary, religious, and various patriotic leaflets stuck here and there on the walls of entryways and telephone poles—from the headlines of articles black with large letters on the front pages of newspapers and journals—from everywhere the artist heard that lightsound sowing unprecedented horror around the world. It was incomprehensible to him why, at just the moment when it would seem that no one was afraid of anything, he had to live with the continual sensation of fear. Why, in every word read in the newspaper and heard on the radio, on the television, from the lips of the orators on the squares and the women in the streets, did he hear a portent of tragedy? Why did his heart darken at the sight of pregnant women or young couples walking in the parks and on the Boulevard? Was it possible that it fell only to him to fear for the future of all people? What had so frightened him once that he now walked in horror at the thought that that roar of the streets and squares sooner or later would bring a new Master to power? Why, exactly, was he, Sadai Sadygly, fated to experience the pain and suffering of inevitable bloodshed now, before it had happened?

Not finding answers to the questions tormenting him, Sadai Sadygly saw Aylis every night in his dreams. Because Aylis was the unhealed wound of his heart. And Sadai, who in any case was inclined to fall into a depressive-melancholy state from time to time, began to shun the world and people more and more each day. He often raved in his sleep, moaned. In his incoherent monologues he mentioned the names of Aikanush, Aniko, Jamal, Lyusik, Babash, and many other people known and unknown to Azada *khanum*.

Once, when Azada *khanum* saw that Sadai, waking up in the middle of the night, crossed himself, she couldn't recover her composure for quite some time.

In one of those nightmare-filled nights, her husband brought up the Aylis fox cub long forgotten by everyone else in his incoherent monologues. Her husband moaned so much in his sleep that Azada *khanum*, who often hid Sadai's aiments from her father, couldn't avoid sharing her anxiety with Dr. Abasaliev the next day.

"Maybe you can talk with him, Papa? Find out what torments him?"

Dr. Abasaliev, who understood quite well that such psychological conditions are not at all a medical problem, tried to calm his daughter.

"It's cryptomnesia," he said. "It's found in all emotional people; as they age, they 'fall into childhood.' Don't be alarmed. One way or another, everyone lives his life."

But the sad thing was precisely that Sadai Sadygly wasn't living his life now. It was strange: Sadai Sadygly, in whose family there was no one with a drop of Armenian blood (one of his grandfathers had made a pilgrimage to Karbala, the other to Mecca), for some time had apparently carried within himself a kind of nameless Armenian. More precisely, hadn't carried but hidden. And with every Armenian beaten, offended, and killed in that giant city, it was as if he himself had been beaten, offended, and killed. Since the beginning of autumn he probably hadn't smiled once, and he'd walked around dispirited and gloomy. He completely forgot the theater, where earlier he'd gone at least twice a week. Even rallies, which at one time he gladly attended, lost all interest for him now. He felt restless in town and didn't know any peace at home.

On one of those windy, rainy evenings he came home in such a state that Azada *khanum* almost shrieked in horror. It was as if someone had plunged him into a pool—all his clothes were wet, and water was pouring from his hair and his chin and from the pockets of his raincoat. His pants were smeared with filth; the buttons on his jacket and shirt collar had been torn off.

Weeping, Azada *khanum* undressed her husband and sat him in a bath of warm water. She gave him a shot of brandy and brought tea. And only when Sadai came to himself did she set about questioning him.

"Where did you fight?"

"I didn't fight."

"Then who did this to you?"

Sadai didn't say anything. But after a long silence he wept so bitterly that Azada *khanum* regretted her question.

"Azia, they set a young woman on fire at the train station! They poured gasoline on her and burned her alive."

"Who set her on fire?" asked Azada *khanum*, wiping away tears.

"Women, Azia. A crowd of street traders. As if they weren't people but a horde of actual jinns."

"Women did this to you?"

The artist was surprised because he really hadn't noticed the state he'd come home in.

"I don't know. I wasn't able to understand anything. When those she-devils set that Armenian on fire and immediately disappeared, I saw that I was standing in the train station alone."

And then he began to relate another thing so upsetting that Azada *khanum* felt very uneasy.

"Last night I dreamed they gave money to some Armenian to kill me."

"Who? Who's planning to kill you?!" cried Azada *khanum*, unable to control herself, in a voice that wasn't her own.

"Our people gave money to that Armenian, the ones in authority now."

"Wake up! There hasn't been any kind of authority here for a long time. And if there is any authority, then it's what's sowing the seeds of enmity everywhere. Do you think the people arranged that hellish nightmare in Sumgait? No, my dear, no! It was arranged by the KGB or possibly the remnants of the authorities who've now separated into the various mafia groups. I'll never believe, Sadai, that Azerbaijanis could come to such senseless wildness without a real, live organizer."

"How can you say such a thing? You were in Aylis, too," said the artist, glancing piercingly, sadly at his wife, and immediately he hung his head, like a child.

"Yes, I was in Aylis, and I know the Turks dealt brutally and cruelly with innocent people there. But you've also been in those places from which *Armenians* drove out thousands of unfortunate *Azerbaijanis*. Have you thought even once about how it is for those unfortunate people, those Azerbaijanis, homeless now and living without the slightest hope for the future? Do our Azerbaijani instigators, the ones who stirred up this bloody trouble, really think about them, the Azerbaijanis whom the unfortunate Armenians themselves now curse? I mean both the Karabakh Armenians and the local Baku Armenians who don't care about us because, according to their thinking, we're also Turks? If the Turks slaughtered your people, go ahead, fight it out with them, why are we Azerbaijanis even involved? In what way are those Armenian screamers better than our homegrown ones? Why don't you think about that, my dear?

Since all this began, you haven't been yourself. Do you know how emaciated you've become, sweetheart? If you won't take pity on yourself, then at least take pity on me. This is not acceptable, Sadai, understand? You won't change anything in this world, just thoroughly destroy yourself. You say you went to the train station? And what did you do there, sweetheart?"

"I wanted. . . I wanted. . . I want to die, Azia," he uttered, with difficulty.

Azada *khanum*, understanding that her husband was on the edge of madness, fell silent.

Sadai Sadygly, retreating into himself for good, was now fully estranged from both his wife and from all earthly things in general. Azada *khanum* understood why her husband went to the train station. For entire days Sadai hung around there just to meet and see off the Baku-Yerevan train known to him since childhood. On that train, which passed through his native Ordubad, he traveled every day in his thoughts, cherishing a crazy new dream about Echmiadzin, where he planned to go to convert to the Christian faith.

The Young Author of a Play in Which Sadai Sadygly Will Never Perform Accuses the Former Master of the Country of Ethical-Moral Genocide against His Own People

Perhaps Sadai Sadygly had again been dreaming of those wonderful summer days spent in Aylis with Dr. Abasaliev. Or perhaps the voice of his father-in-law, which he'd heard the previous night on the telephone from Mardakan, still sounded in the artist's ears. In any case, just as soon as Sadai awoke that morning, it seemed to him that the whole world was filled with the ringing, bright voice of Professor Abasaliev. And continuing to hear that bright, ringing voice, Sadai felt more cheerful and peaceful than he'd ever felt before; it seemed it was easier for him to bear his pain in a world where the voice of Dr. Abasaliev could still be heard.

It was the next-to-last Saturday in 1989. About an hour had passed since Azada *khanum* had gone to work, and hardly had she left the house than the phone began to ring. For more than an hour it rang at five- to ten-minute intervals, but Sadai didn't pick up the receiver.

In the pauses between the rings, the artist heard a cloyingly sweet voice in his ears, and before his eyes stood the well-known figure of Maupassant Miralamov, the director of the theater, from whose lips floated lines by a well-known poet of the people:

> We greet the Great Master,
> The Equal of Eternity![3]

For more than a week now, the director had phoned Sadai Sadygly every day and, instead of greeting him, each time repeated those lines—disgusting in their triteness—that evoked an almost physical nausea in him.

Finally, Sadai had to pick up the receiver.

This time it wasn't Maupassant Miralamov but Nuvarish Karabakhly.

"Brother, why don't you pick up the phone?" he asked in his quiet, wheezy voice. "I've already called you fifty times. I'm sick with worry—I keep thinking something's happened. Your fellow villager arrived here, someone from your hometown—your child-hood friend Jamal."

"He arrived where?" Sadai asked this with such amazement that he was frightened by his own voice.

"He's here, in the theater. Come quickly, he's waiting for you." Nuvarish Karabakhly paused for a second and added, "He's in Maupassant *muallim*'s office."

If Nuvarish Karabakhly said "Maupassant *muallim*," then he really was phoning from the director's office. Otherwise, he would have called the director something different: behind the director's back, everyone called him Uncle Moposh.

"I'm coming," answered Sadai Sadygly. However, he lacked the strength to move from where he was.

Since the time Jamal had become a shepherd after the seventh grade, Sadai hadn't seen him once. But he always remembered him. Moreover, recently he'd been obsessed with the idea of going to the village to find Jamal there in the mountains, no matter what it took, and finally asking him: on that day after Aikanush washed his head in the churchyard, had the whole world really been lit up with such a velvety-soft, yellow-rose light or had it seemed that way to Sadai alone? But now that the real possibility of seeing Jamal had appeared, it turned into a heavy burden.

When he finally left the house and was already getting into a taxi, the thought suddenly entered his head that Jamal's arrival might not be a fact but a clever trick of the sharp Maupassant Miralamov. In fact, for a long time the director had been trying to lure him to the theater by various ruses and absolutely force him to read a play he'd already lavished praise on for many days over the phone. It was indeed possible that Moposh wasn't making this up, that the lead role in the play had, in fact, been specially written for him, Sadai. And it was fully possible that the eternal optimist, the businesslike, quick-witted Maupassant hoped that Sadai Sadygly playing the lead role would put the dying theater back on its feet. That was his character; if he undertook something, he was bound to carry it through to the end. And to discover that Sadai had once had a childhood friend named Jamal wouldn't have presented great difficulty for Moposh—the director might have heard about it from Sadai himself and remembered. In any case, this was the truth: the artist now riding in the taxi didn't have any particular desire to meet with Jamal.

However, it turned out that Jamal really had arrived.

Looking serious, dressed in a cheap, new suit and wearing an expensive Bukhara *papakha* on his head, he'd made himself comfortable in the warm and cozy office of Maupassant Miralamov. His face had been tanned a shade of copper in the mountains, and his large, hazel eyes shone from the agitation and excitement elicited by unfamiliar conditions.

Sadai didn't see Nuvarish Karabakhly in the office. He'd probably gone to rehearsal, Sadai decided, or to film something somewhere in the television studio. (Sadai didn't know that for a long time now Nuvarish, being preoccupied with the search for a pistol, had been sitting around waiting in vain in various reception rooms of important people.)

Seeing Sadai, Maupassant Miralamov leaped up from his armchair with unexpected agility for his age, threw himself on the artist, embraced him right at the door, and clasped him firmly to his bosom. He was even able to squeeze a tear from his eye in an attempt to demonstrate how happy he was to see him.

Jamal puckered his lips naïvely, like a child, clearly preparing to kiss his classmate warmly. Sadai clasped the head of his friend to his bosom, along with the stylish *papakha*. For several seconds they looked at one another in silence. And those short seconds were enough for Jamal to collect his thoughts, decide how to start the conversation, and even to become a little emotional at first and then burst into tears—loudly, with sobs.

"I'm in a terrible mess, brother!" he said. "I came to ask for your help. My son has been arrested and put in jail. There's not a single office in the district on whose door I haven't knocked. No one wants to hear me out. So I came here, maybe I can find help here."

"And why did they arrest your son?" the artist asked irritably; clearly, he didn't like the fact that Jamal was crying like a woman.

Jamal didn't answer. Pulling a handkerchief from his pocket, he painstakingly wiped away the tears and sweat that had appeared on his brow. Then, finally coming to himself, he began to tell the story in a now-quiet and calm voice.

"It's Divine punishment for my stupidity, Sary. What a fool I was to take the granddaughter of that butcher Mamedaga as a daughter-in-law, to mix my blood with the blood of that rotten breed. And

I'm suffering now. She just rides roughshod over me, and she attacks her mother-in-law like a mad dog. She only knows how to growl, quarrel, and put a curse on things.

"She's disgraced us before the whole village. And then she caught up a sharp cleaver and hit herself in the head: what a bitch! And at the instigation of her father, Jinn-Eye Shaban, she rushed to town, to the hospital, she says, 'Look, people, my husband wanted to kill me!' She slandered the boy and had him arrested. And for twenty days now, I've left no stone unturned. I've been to everyone in the district; no one wants to even listen. I've lost every hope. All my hope is on you, Sadai. You can help me. After all, you're a famous person." Jamal fell silent, fastening his gaze full of mildness on Sadai.

Sadai began to pity Jamal. At the same time, he experienced tremendous sympathy for himself and for Aylis, even for that crazy, quarrelsome daughter of Jinn-Eye Shaban. Aylis was grey this season, the mountains were grey. Freezing, hardly breathing from the cold, the stones, streets, and houses were waiting for the arrival of spring. The Stone Church. That same *qanat* spring, the most powerful in Aylis, flowing out from beneath its stone walls, its water running now under the icy irrigation canals and turning a little bit black, mixing with some nameless fear; that same miraculous black fox cub—God's little creation. And also that scarlet spot of blood, stiffening forever on the stone fence by the spring there, where Jinn-Eye Shaban had shot it. Looking into the grey and pitiful face of Aylis, the artist was suddenly ashamed with his whole heart that he'd ever wanted to ask Jamal about the yellow-rose light.

"We'll see. We'll think up something," Sadai Sadygly answered uncertainly, without any hope, and added, a bit louder, "Well, tell me, what's new in Aylis?"

"What could possibly be new in Aylis? Everything's exactly the way you saw it," Jamal replied, with extreme reluctance.

"Do you know how many years it's been since I was in Aylis?"

"Say it's been a hundred. If you didn't come to Aylis for a hundred years, nothing would change," answered Jamal, and for some reason he smiled pitifully at just Maupassant. Then, apparently deciding that he had to tell Sadai something or other about Aylis, he said unwillingly, "This year Mirali *kishi* died at the end of winter, you probably heard about that. And the other day Anykh also gave her unclean soul to Azrail. And there was so much anger in that old woman—she remained an Armenian even on the threshold of death. When our old women went to say goodbye to her, she announced to them, she said, 'I didn't even think about changing my faith, and I never renounced my God. That means that to this very minute I was actually pulling the wool over your eyes, to put it in polite terms.' How vile these Armenians are!" Jamal comically wrinkled up his face, and again he looked meekly and warily at Maupassant Miralamov. Then he turned his gaze on Sadai and in some kind of strange confusion hung his head.

"So now it's fashionable in Aylis for people to spread lunacy about Armenians?" asked Sadai in a constrained voice that could barely be heard. He tried to imagine Aniko, the last Armenian of Aylis, on her death bed, surrounded by the Aylis Muslim women in the hour of her death.

But he wasn't able to imagine the scene of her death. He could see the big, two-story house, the best in Aylis. The tall veranda filled with flowers of all different kinds. The solid stone steps leading up to it, pleasing the eye with their irreproachable cleanliness and neatness. In Sadai's eyes, the world was made much brighter by Aniko's multicolored flowers, grown by her in the yard of the Vang Church and cared for by her year round. Glancing at Jamal's expensive *papakha*, the artist remembered his dirty, lice-ridden cap that Aikanush had once taken from his head in fear.

"If you had a God, you wouldn't have betrayed him, either!" he said loudly and pitilessly. And immediately thereafter (either from regret about what he'd said, or for some other reason), he felt a terrible emptiness in his soul—some sort of boundless, hopeless ruin, without life and without air. In the brief moment of silence arising after his words, he was able to see a suspiciously reproachful, cold smile in the eyes of Maupassant Miralamov; the clean-shaven, well-fed face of the director had suddenly turned grey. However—just think!—Sadai's angry words didn't offend Jamal in the least.

"You're absolutely right," he answered. "Armenians are always in harmony with their God."

The words seemed painfully familiar to Sadai. The artist heard them not just as words but as some forgotten sound, as a gentle, kind light that had existed at one time in this world and then disappeared without a trace. In some miraculous way, Sadai Sadygly found peace and consolation for himself in those words. He was prepared to rifle his entire memory to recall from whom, when, and where he'd first heard them. He wanted to embrace, to press all Aylis to his bosom like one communal house, to rock it like a small sapling, to gather it in his cupped hand and drink it like a swallow of water so that he could remember from whom in Aylis he might first have heard that most simple—and at the same time, unbelievably profound— phrase spoken just now by Jamal.

Your secrets are inscrutable, Lord—couldn't those words really once have been spoken by True Majesty Itself, inscrutable Aylis? "Armenians are always in harmony with their God."

Rejoicing sincerely, Sadai embraced Jamal about the shoulders.

"Ah, you're still Jambul—Jambul! Look how honest you turned out to be. You didn't take offense. After all, I insulted you."

"An honest man is never offended by honest words!" said Jamal, enunciating every word grandly. "It is said: Better to be the slave of an honest word than the lord of a lie."

"This is your first time in Baku?"

"No, I've been a couple of times. And one of my daughters got married and moved here."

"To whom have you left the mountains while you're away?" Sadai asked, joking.

"Who could threaten the Master of the mountains?" Jamal answered seriously, meaning God, of course.

"You don't look after sheep anymore?"

"I do, why wouldn't I? I have tons of grandsons in Aylis. They can certainly manage the place without me."

Sadai stood up and began to pace around the office. "So, what should we do?"

"About what?"

"About jail, what should we do about that?"

As if he'd been waiting for just that moment, Maupassant Miralamov stood up.

"What's so complicated? You'll write a nice little note to the district public prosecutor, and our brother will give it to him. The public prosecutor won't refuse you. They'll release the boy, and that's the end of it." The director winked stealthily at Sadai Sadygly and held out paper and pen towards him, already prepared. "What right does a prosecutor have to not listen to the word of a famous People's Artist?" (In unofficial situations he always called Sadai Sadygly a People's Artist.) "Moreover, nobody's killed anyone. So, something happened, they fought, they quarreled. So, they'll reconcile, that's it." The director again winked surreptitiously, slyly at Sadai, and only now did the artist understand that Moposh simply wanted to get rid of Jamal as quickly as possible.

"No, that won't do. What will my letter matter to the prosecutor if he can get some money out of someone else?" The artist resolutely crumpled up the paper that had been extended to him, giving the director to understand that he didn't agree with his charade. And glancing at Jamal's sad, worried face, he saw dim, sunless, dismal, dead, dreary Aylis once more in the depths of his heart. Aylis, which had lost the greatness of its mountains and of its churches, which were just as great. The grey streets with no people. The dead yards that lay bare after autumn. The lifeless trees left without a single leaf, the ruined mountains—without shepherds and without sheep. Only grey crows flew in the grey, dead sky over the grey Muslim cemetery. Feeling a terrible hopelessness, after long deliberation Sadai said, "Maybe we should track down Babash?"

Jamal cheered up and instantly came to life.

"Yes!" he exclaimed excitedly. "Let's find him! He'll surely help me. He has an important job, honor, respect—Babash has it all." He leaped up from the desk. "You just lead me to him. I'll take care of the rest."

Sadai Sadygly had heard plenty about Babash's big career achievements. After a short stint in the central committee of the Komsomol, he'd immediately gotten a job as chair of the district executive committee of one of the large districts in Baku. He was the first secretary of the district Party committee and for a long time even occupied a minister's chair. Recently Babash had been head of a department of the Central Committee, and only two months ago a new organization had been created, the Society of Those Who Are Dedicated to the People, whose president Babash Ziyadov had become.

Having avoided contact with Babash for many years, Sadai was now prepared to do anything for Jamal. However, he didn't know exactly where the organization led by Babash was located. In spite of this, he decided without hesitation to throw himself into the search. Concerned by this decisiveness, the director began bustling about and ran out from behind the desk, not letting them leave the office.

"Where are you going?" exclaimed Moposh, blocking the exit. "Do you mean your fellow villager Babash Ziyadov? Then wait a minute. Let's phone, inquire. Maybe he's out."

On the director's desk sat three telephones, not outwardly distinguishable from one another: an internal line, a local line, and a third line for just three-digit numbers—a private government line. The fact that Moposh picked up the receiver of that third line was reflected on his face, which all of a sudden became detached and serious. Cleary demonstrating his own importance, he dialed three numbers. However, hearing the voice of Babash Ziyadov, he couldn't hide his confusion.

"Hello, Babash Bilalovich! This is Miralamov. . . Yes, from the theater. . . Yes, and God grant you the same. . . Endlessly grateful. . . There will be. We have a fantastic play. . . He himself? Yes, of course, He knows. Yes, yes, He's aware. . . He acquainted himself personally with the play. . . He liked it. Liked it a lot. . . Yes, the subject is extremely topical. . . His image? It is, it is. Yes, the whole play's about the shameful excesses he committed here for thirty years. . . In the lead role? Yes, yes, it is he. Your fellow villager, our pride and joy. Actually, the author wrote that role specifically for Sadai *muallim*. And He himself said He'd like to see Sadai Sadygly in that role. Yes, yes, He himself."

Sadai Sadygly knew that with the rise of the new First Person to power, a campaign was unfolding everywhere to unmask the former, already disgraced leader. By the way the director suddenly sprang from his chair and began to thank Babash, the artist understood that Babash Ziyadov had promised the theater something. Undoubtedly, Babash had guessed that Sadai was now in the director's office. However, true to bureaucratic etiquette, Maupassant was waiting until Ziyadov himself expressed the wish to speak with the artist. And finally that long-awaited moment arrived.

"Yes, he's here, right next to me, wants to say hello to you." And Moposh, almost dancing from happiness, handed the receiver to Sadai.

After greeting Babash, the artist immediately got down to business.

"Jamal's arrived," he said drily. "He has business with you."

"Is it really that difficult a thing?" Babash tried to joke.

"Not difficult for you."

"Then why is it difficult for you, great artist? Is it possible people respect you less than they respect us?"

"If I were able to help, I wouldn't have bothered to phone you." Sadai tried to be as friendly as possible. "So, will you see him?"

Apparently, Babash Ziyadov had quickly understood that joking with the artist wouldn't lead to anything good, and after a short pause, he answered in a now-serious tone.

"Fine, send him over, I'll see him." Then he was silent again and, with ill-disguised injury in his voice, added, "I thought you phoned to congratulate me."

With those words Babash hung up the phone, while the artist stood with the receiver in his hand, looking uncomprehendingly at Maupassant Miralamov.

"Did you hear? He says, 'You didn't congratulate me.' What was I supposed to congratulate him for?"

"I don't know. . ." muttered the director thoughtfully, not lifting his eyes from the telephone. "A big article came out in yesterday's *Kommunist*. Probably he's thinking of that."

"He's also become a writer?!" growled the artist, and he headed towards the door after Jamal, who was leaving the office.

"Where are you going?!" yelled Maupassant with unexpected rudeness.

"To show him the way—he won't find it on his own."

"Sit down. My driver will take him." Practically shoving Jamal out of the office, Miralamov seized hold of Sadai's arm, led him over, and sat him in an armchair. "Listen, what's going on with you?" he said in a sorrowful voice, clearly pitying the artist.

"What do you mean?"

"For a whole month I haven't been able to drag you out of your house."

"Don't exaggerate, it hasn't been a month," responded Sadai Sadygly.

"When were you last here? If you remember, I owe you a good *khash*."

"Honestly, Moposh, I'm tired, everything is repulsive to me," confessed the artist sincerely.

"Why are you so tired? Who repulses you? When did anyone here treat you badly? But you lock yourself up and sit at home. I don't understand, what can you possibly do at home for days on end?"

Miralamov took a key from the pocket of his jacket and unhurriedly began to open the little door of an ancient locker masked as a safe—in the theater they called it Moposh's hidey hole. From there he extracted a bottle of French cognac reserved for the most important visitors, a box of Moscow bonbons, and two crystal shot glasses and stood them on the desk.

"Well, let's sit down," he said, pouring cognac into the shot glasses. "Let's sit a while, relax."

Sadai Sadygly hadn't drunk a drop of alcohol in many months. He'd somehow convinced himself that if he drank, he'd surely cause some kind of trouble. Moreover, some kind of terrible trouble. However, the cognac he was drin ing freed him here and now from that fear. A pleasant, aromatic warmth spread over his body, penetrated his soul, was absorbed in his blood. And everything around him unexpectedly became wider, freer, kinder.

And why, my God, in an Aylis long forgotten by You, did all Your mountains and stones come to life again? And, Lord, how was the voice of Aniko, gone now into non-being, able to create one more bright, living, and sonorous Aylis morning out of nothing? And why, Creator, did Sadai suddenly want so badly to praise and glorify Aniko in front of Maupassant Miralamov—to speak about the love of hard work and uprightness of the last Armenian woman to inhabit Aylis?

The passionate wish to say some lofty words to the theater director about the Aylis Armenians in general, about their marvelously creative love of hard work and never-ending faith in God, rose in the artist. However, he didn't do that. He understood there was no point in talking about any one of the Aylis Armenians to a person not born in Aylis, a person who had no conception of the ringing of bells from the twelve Aylis churches when it sounded all at once; who hadn't heard anything about the black horse of Adif Bey or the sharp dagger of Mamedaga the butcher; who hadn't once seen that yellow-rose light shining mysteriously on the high cupola of the church that might to this very day bewitch the soul of some young Aylis boy.

No, he didn't say a single word to Maupassant Miralamov about Aylis. Instead, he praised Moposh's cognac and said nice things about the bonbons. And in his soul he thought there was no purpose in persistently avoiding people. Loneliness, he thought, is death, and possibly even worse than death. And he also thought that, in any event, it was good to drink a little now and then; otherwise, it was possible to leave this life without having escaped its sticky melancholy.

After a shot of French cognac, Maupassant Miralamov's mood also visibly improved. His face cleared, and his eyes shone. But "Uncle Moposh," who was impatient to talk about the new play, didn't hurry at all to get to business. Perhaps he wished first (according to plan) to improve the artist's mood, so as to persuade him more easily later. But perhaps he dragged his feet for fear of hearing a refusal from Sadai Sadygly, whose character he knew very well. Or else the director himself wasn't certain of the artistic merits of the play sent to the theater from the Central Committee, and therefore now, under friendly conditions, it was hard for him to lavish praise on it as convincingly as he'd done more than once in phone conversations with the artist.

Maupassant Miralamov again poured cognac into the shot glasses. Sipping in small mouthfalls, he smiled, shining all over from happiness.

"Look, Master, how well everything has turned out! It seems God is favorably inclined towards me, too, although I'm not nearly the saint my best friend Sadai Sadygly is. God did all this. And Allah himself sent your shepherd here today. If he hadn't come, I might not have been able to lure you from home for another month. And how excellently things turned out with Ziyadov. What reason would I have had to phone Ziyadov if your childhood friend hadn't showed up here in the flesh? You heard how I charmed him with the name of the new First Person? Ziyadov is already prepared to finance three or four showings of our next play. And he will finance it, I'm one-hundred-percent sure of it. He's back on the horse now. He made friends with the new First Person when he worked in the Komsomol."

"But wasn't Babash a person of the former First Person?" Sadai Sadygly asked artlessly, all his thoughts focused on Jamal.

"Drink," proposed the director, nodding at the shot glass standing in front of Sadai. "It's real balm. I have excellent tea, we'll make some now." He got up, filled the electric samovar with water, and plugged it into the socket. "Stop it, for the love of God! Did the former First Person ever really want to see another living person as his equal? Who would have dared say 'I'm also a person, the son of such-and-such a man or such-and-such a woman' in front of him? With his gendarme methods he could turn anybody—if there was anything human left in that person—into any kind of beast, so long as that person humbly served him. He compelled everyone, without exception, to wear a mask on his face. How can we say now which of those people were his people and which weren't?"

Sadai Sadygly remembered how Moposh himself had bowed and scraped in front of the former First Person some ten years ago in this very office and barely stopped himself from uttering a colorful oath. He drained the cognac and stood the shot glass on the desk.

"Stop, stop, have you no shame?" he exclaimed. "You're saying this to me?!"

The artist's sudden outburst plunged Maupassant into confusion, took him down a peg.

"If not to you, then with whom can I share this now, my brother?" he said in a plaintive voice. "I'm telling the truth, isn't that so? If all of those had really been his people, then at least someone among them would have gone to visit him now at least once. But they say no one goes near him. He sits by himself in the dacha and moans and groans from loneliness."

"Of course he moans and groans, who wouldn't moan and groan?" Getting up from his seat, the artist began pacing around the room. "Those people in whose faces he spat—with the spittle still fresh—have already lined up to lick the butt of the new First Person, as you pompously name him, either from 'love' or from fear."

Maupassant wasn't able to hide his embarrassment; all the same, he collected himself and found something to answer.

"Yes, that's so, you're absolutely right. And we are like that, both I and that Babash Ziyadov. But that's really his legacy, brother mine. You know, for thirteen years we watched him convert servility into a way of life for the whole country. Can a new First Person really change anything in a couple of years?" Maupassant even turned red from agitation. "But everything will be put to rights, you'll see, step by step everything will change."

"No, nothing will change," said Sadai Sadygly feverishly, excitedly. "And you won't do anything to hurt the former Master, as they call him to this day among the people, even if you revile him still more loudly. Now you plan to pile all the guilt for your own servile obedience on him so as to get out of that shit with clean hands. You crave a little bloodletting and are in a terrible hurry for it because you want everything immediately, and more of it, and—most importantly— without expending energy or intelligence. But, look, he reached such heights thanks to his own intelligence. And an innate passion for power supplied his energy. Yes, he composed servile hymns, but didn't you sing them in unison? And now, at the very height of corruption, when not a drop of conscience or shame remains in people, when insult and malice suffocate everyone, when lies have become so widespread it's difficult not to lose your bearings, you've found the 'boldness' in yourself to present the bill to the disgraced Master." Having fallen aloofly silent, he then continued, harshly and adamantly, as before, "But he deserves respect, if only because he had a clear life's goal, even if it was a police-strongman's goal. He was a person of living, flexible intelligence and unbelievable quickness. A person who always knew precisely what he needed. And he was damnably strong, to boot." The artist spoke loudly, and he'd already ceased being angry; on the contrary, he exulted in a restrained way.

Maupassant Miralamov sat without moving. Having known the artist well for a long time, he'd probably assumed in advance that Sadai Sadygly wouldn't go against the disgraced former Leader, wouldn't stand for singing in one choir with his new-minted opponents—that would have been against his character. But what the artist said alarmed him.

"Look at this, look at this," he muttered, dismayed. "To tell the truth, I thought as much. I knew you wouldn't swim with the current." Maupassant spoke gently and amicably, trying to appear respectable. "You endured much evil from him, but you don't want to answer evil with evil. At the same time, such scrupulousness would do you honor if we were talking now about an ordinary person who'd been undeservedly offended. But we're talking about a state official. Therefore I'm inclined to think you've succumbed to your emotions. You know you didn't think this way just two or three months ago when we were meeting a minimum of once a week in the theater."

"Yes, we were meeting," answered Sadai Sadygly, screwing up his eyes in suffering, eyes that were red from excitement. "But I had more than enough in those two to three months to clearly imagine where all this *perestroika* yapping and all this political stirring are leading the country. I'm convinced that only supremely untalented people could so talentlessly ruin the country. Do you really not see that there's no clear thinking in any one of their actions? And all of their *perestroika* is nothing more than a new weapon in the struggle for power. The people are in complete confusion, and no one believes he's master of his own fate. Everything's going to pieces and being ruined. The country's becoming a stinking swamp. A pack of quarreling dogs intoxicated with cheap freedom, competing day and night in empty, pointless chatter. A lot of water will have to go under the bridge for these insatiable talkers to want to even hear one another." The artist spoke passionately, as if he were onstage wishing to be heard in the last row. "And instead of considering and comprehending the meaning of what's happened, your new First Person and his friend from the Komsomol are hurrying to kick the former First Person in the teeth just for the trite and banal reason that when he was in power, they trudged along at the tail of power for a long time, although they received even that power from his hand." The artist again grew irritable, and excitement caught in his throat. "Yes, he collected toadies around himself and periodically mocked them publicly. But as I now understand, he did it because he knew for sure: in the depths of his soul, every toady is a potential tyrant. And in every such petty tyrant he saw a pitiful parody of himself. But all that was yesterday. And is today any better? They've turned the country into an enormous insane asylum. Even the Kremlin resembles a fly-by-night operation without a guard where self-described political wunderkinds get carried away with their schemes, driving the country into a dead end. They test the people, promising them some kind of illusory *perestroika* miracles, and what really happens? Everybody runs wild. Fires blaze all around, and a handful of sharp thugs with dull consciences irresponsibly summon people to still greater social activism. Compared to these political shits, I'm prepared to place the former First Person on the level of the greats."

Maupassant Miralamov, who knew dozens of Sadai Sadygly's monologues by heart—monologues spoken from the stage under an avalanche of applause—listened to this one, fascinated, like an experienced theatergoer. Even before this he'd known Sadai Sadygly had long outgrown being an artist, but now he was becoming a bit scared. He wasn't planning to argue with Sadai, but suddenly, it was as if he'd been stung. Gloatingly rubbing his hands, he unexpectedly interrupted the actor.

"Stop, stop! You don't think He himself planned Sumgait to get back at the Kremlin?"

"No, there was no thought of that," Sadai answered without hesitation. "Moreover, I'm absolutely certain that when the people who'd lost their heads from cheap liberty did their black deeds in Sumgait, he was sitting in front of the television at the dacha and weeping bitter tears, horrified at what third-rate politics was doing in this once-exemplary Soviet Socialist Republic."

"Well, just listen to you, my God! As if you've already forgotten what an insufferable person he was. You were just outraged in front of your fellow villager that now anyone who wants to can spread lunacy about Armenians. But you know very well the Armenians turned away from us as the result of his cunning and treacherous politics. And now you pretend none of that happened. You praise him, having decided a debt of honor and decency demands it. And you know he hated you ferociously, everyone knew it."

The artist was stunned by the insincerity of Maupassant's belated boldness.

"O Lord, save me, save me!" he exclaimed loudly. "You're lying again, Moposh—sometimes he was even in sympathy with me. He always had his own interests, I don't deny that. But he never squandered those whom the people valued and respected.

"And as far as how the former First Person related to me personally, he was guilty to exactly the same degree that I was. I lived and breathed hatred towards the system of state security organs then. I wanted to save the honor of Azeri theater all by myself — that's what kind of fool I was! It seems to me now that he somehow sensed and understood my quixotism. Because he himself was quite talented, Moposh!" The artist thought for a minute, annoyed at his fit of temper, then continued in a more restrained way. "He forbade me formal prosperity and cheap glory. He pushed me to mutiny against himself. And I very much liked the role he assigned me in that good-natured tragicomedy. You know, I've always thought it's necessary to periodically spoil one's relationship with authority in order to preserve the feeling of freedom in oneself.

In that regard, I'm prepared to consider him as my godfather."

"Aren't you aware, my dear man, that you unceasingly contradict yourself?" asked Maupassant quietly.

Lit with an inner flame, Sadai Sadygly either didn't hear his retort or else decided to let it go in one ear and out the other.

"But that was then, when I was able to find the strength in myself to get up after any blow. Now I don't have that strength. I don't understand anything now, Moposh, I swear on the grave of my mother. I confess to you, Moposh: I'm afraid. I'm constantly having nightmares, each one more terrible than the last. For a long time I've tried to not have any connection with the external world. And when I collide with it, I'm astounded at what goes on in it. People have changed to the point of being unrecognizable. It's so terrible, Moposh, that there didn't turn out to be a single spiritual authority in the whole country who was able tell people the truth, who was unafraid for his own skin. Where is our humane nation? Where is our celebrated intelligentsia? I've felt that for a long time, Moposh, and I thought about it earlier, too: even without him, the noose our former 'Dear Father' tightened around the throats of the unruly should have at some point strangled our unfortunate intelligentsia." The artist fell silent, experiencing a terrifying devastation within himself.

Maupassant excitedly leaped up from his armchair and exclaimed, "Brother, you're a genius, I swear by Allah! What a terrific monologue you've given. Only, my dear man, am I really arguing? After all, I'm saying the exact same thing."

"No, you're saying: Let's ally ourselves with yet another power-loving Master of the country. So that when he's got nothing better to do, he can come here and amuse himself with us. And you do indeed see that the place of the former Master is empty. All the people have now fastened their gaze on that empty place and with diabolical unease in their souls secretly long for the former First Person. That's where his strength lies. He left such a hole after himself that no one but he can fill it."

This time he himself poured cognac into the shot glasses with shaking hands and, hardly having swallowed, grasped the reason for his unease, which had lodged in some corner of his brain.

"I've been meaning to ask, but I forgot. You said Babash Ziyadov wrote an article. What did he write in it? Is it possible that he, too, is denouncing the former First Person?" he asked sarcastically.

"No, it seems it's not about the former First Person. On the other hand, your fellow villager really sticks it to the Armenians." Maupassant forced himself to smile. "I'll have a look now, it must be here somewhere." He got up and easily pulled the newspaper from a thick pile.

It was a long article, occupying a whole page of the newspaper *Kommunist*.

In the center was a headline composed of giant black letters: "The Vile Armenian Trail," and at the end stood the name of the author—"Babakhan Ziyadkhanly."

Even without his glasses, Sadai Sadygly could make out the phrases "ungrateful people," "treacherous people," and "dangerous enemy" highlighted in thick type and scattered generously throughout the article. He was ready to set the paper aside when his glance came across the word "Istazyn," and then, putting on his glasses, he began to read the whole article.

Before this, the artist had encountered similar appalling vulgarity only, perhaps, in trashy, pseudopopulist articles by newly minted historians and hack writers who'd fallen into full senility. It was clearly apparent from the article that Babash had read an abundance of those kinds of compositions.

According to Babash Ziyadov, the word Istazyn originally meant *usta ozan* ("master" or "preacher"), and Armenians had deliberately distorted it in converting it to their own language, allegedly to erase the traces of the indigenous inhabitants on that land from history. Those same *usta ozans*, he said, had migrated from mountainous Aylis to the land between the Tigris and Euphrates rivers three thousand year before our era—that is, the plains, the *sum er*—and created a state there that was called *Sumer* in their language, thus giving birth to an ancient civilization, now well-known under the name Sumerian.

According to "Babakhan Ziyadkhanly," the word Aylis was formed from the word *ailaj*, meaning "place of settlement." It was as if Armenians had never lived in Aylis and all the churches and the cemeteries had earlier been named *giur od* (wild flame) in the mythical "Odar" language so revered by pan-Turkists—in short, that these had been the lands of ancient Turkic peoples better known as Albanians.[4] The author argued heatedly that our "ungrateful neighbors" had altered the toponymy of the territory of Azerbaijan for the duration of all recorded history, giving it their own names. For example, they named Oderman "Girdiman," Giursa "Goris," Gurbag "Karabakh," and Elvend "Yerevan," giving out that these lands had historically belonged to them. The land called Gapuagyz (entry, gate) in the "Odar" language that subsequently acquired the name "Caucasus" in its Russified form was the land of the ancient "Ermens"—courageous Turkic men. However (he said), our neighbors took their name precisely from that word, which is how the heretofore non-existent Armenian people arose here in the Caucasus.

Babash concluded his lengthy article with lines from the poet Ulurukh Turanmekan (whose name means "the supreme being of the Turan lands"), lines well known to all and already becoming the hymn of a new time:

> *Dearer than blood, dearer than life:*
> *Azerbaijan—our home—is that pearl.*
> *Only a coward, an out-and-out scoundrel*
> *Wouldn't give blood or life for her.*

Reading Babash's nonsense, the artist's mind wandered around Aylis, street after little street, house after house, from Istazyn (Astvatsadun) to Vuragyrd, and having finished the article, for some reason he suddenly thought he'd never see Aylis again, never pass through its gardens and streets.

Before his eyes rose the solitary grave of his mother in the Muslim cemetery of Aylis. During the last week his mother had come to Sadai every night in a dream. She sat near his bed trying to speak with him, but each time she rose silently and left. Why was she silent, with what was she displeased? Sadai didn't dare ask her about it. More precisely, he couldn't—he was struck dumb before his mother. And each time he woke up, he thought that perhaps his mother was displeased and worried precisely because in his soul he so thirsted for Echmiadzin. He couldn't imagine any other reason for his mother's displeasure.

And suddenly it seemed to him that Aylis itself had never existed in the world. There had never been a Babash or a Jamal or a Lyusik. There had never been that church or that yellow-rose light that reminded him of the smile of the Almighty. And swallowing the lump in his throat, he thought that maybe even God was an invention, a lie. That He doesn't exist and had never been.

"Since when has our Babash Ziyadov become 'Babakhan Ziyadkhanly'?" he asked, his face dark. "In Aylis, one of his grandfathers was a half-educated mullah, and the other was a clown who ran a tearoom."

Maupassant smirked, looking around himself in confusion.

"Look how that scumbag has taken off," Sadai Sadygly continued. "No conscience and no shame. What the insatiable thirst for power can do to a person! That Asskhan Pussykhanly has found himself a whole arsenal of choice lies to slander his hometown, but he hasn't found one word of compassion for his very own godfather. And you know, God didn't make that Asskhan out of clay, Moposh, it was actually our Leader who made him." He sat down, devastated, enveloped in despair and despondency. "And now, be so good as to tell me: who authorized Babash Ziyadov to publish such stinking shit in the official Party newspaper, and why did he sign that shit not as Babash Ziyadov but 'Babakhan Ziyadkhanly'? What khan did he descend from? There's never been a bey or khan in the lineage of that mongrel."

"What can I say?" Moposh forced himself to say after an extended pause. "Probably they advised him to sign it that way. So they decided to do it that way."

"Who decided?"

"Oh, those at the top. Where else are those questions decided?"

"What, up there at the top they're planning to start a war? If Babash is their person why, in his article—if one may call it an article—did he so unthinkingly, like an irresponsible 'rally patriot,' pour oil on the fire?"

The director decided that the moment had obviously arrived to demonstrate his intelligence and statesmanship to the artist.

"Your naïveté kills me, to be honest! Do you really not see what these conjurers, these 'front line soldiers' screaming 'Karabakh, Karabakh!' everywhere are up to? They don't give a damn about

Karabakh. Their goal is to topple the authorities and take power in their own hands.

"And now the mob on the street only listens to those who curse Armenians. What's the government supposed to do in such a situation? They also need to play the Armenian card for their own ends. That's politics, Master. And politics is a multifaceted thing." And Maupassant smiled, clearly proud of his own intelligence.

"Yes, yes, really important politics. Dear God, it's simply genius! So, the mobs got lucky again—look at all those opportunities opened up for baseness. It's possible to do any dirty trick, the Armenians will be guilty in the end, all the same." The artist walked right up to the director and looked him straight in the eye. "Now, Moposh, let's talk, man to man: if your play is dedicated to such 'political ingenuity,' then you can consider it already decided that I refuse to do it. I'm not of an age to propagandize that kind of nonsense and vulgarity from the stage."

If Maupassant Miralamov could have seen anyone else in the lead role of the play on whose success he'd pinned such great hopes, then perhaps he might have disregarded the author's request and even the wish of the leadership and fired this overly fastidious person on the spot. But the fact of the matter was that he himself could only see Sadai Sadygly in that role.

"You say extraordinary things," he said. "Does it really become me to use cunning with you in these matters?" He dragged a folder from a drawer of the desk and held it out to the artist. "Here's the play *We Called Hell Heaven*. It's perfectly clear from the name what it's about. You yourself at one time told us all this, only we didn't have the intelligence to understand. And now, a young author has appeared, having written a play about it. In it, he creates a negative portrait of the Leader as quite a political adventurist." The director fell silent and thought for a little while. "Such a great artist as you has never received the title of People's Artist. Why? Because you always spoke the truth. You never bowed down before that political dragon. And now, a thousand times glory to Allah, everything is gradually changing. And the new First Person knows you well. He knows you're one of the few in the intelligentsia who didn't sing dithyrambs to the Leader. So, immediately after the premier you'll receive the title you earned long ago. It's all arranged."

It seemed Maupassant Miralamov wanted to cast a spell over Sadai Sadygly. And anyone watching them might have thought the director was succeeding. Because the artist, it appeared, listened submissively and meekly to Maupassant in silence. In fact, Sadai Sadygly was just tired. Now there was no difference at all for him between the former First Person and the new First Person, Moposh and Babash, Jambul Jamal and Jinn-Eye Shaban, between fact and fiction, the truth and a lie. It seemed to him that everything around him was steeped in falsehood and corruption. And still, some kind of feeling of shame and regret that refused to be explained pitilessly pursued the artist. What did he regret so painfully? Perhaps that he'd talked too much with Moposh who, even after everything that had happened, hadn't learned anything and as of old, tried to be a lifeless backdrop of the political court-theater. Or perhaps Jamal had left that bottomless emptiness of soul in his wake—such a pathetic and practical person, not having anything in common with that yellow-rose church light and their shared childhood in Aylis. Or was he feeling so grieved and anxious because in his mind he'd seen the new face of Eternal Evil, which had acquired a new name—Babakhan Ziyadkhanly?

One way or another, after his wearisome, hours-long conversation with Maupassant Miralamov the day before that tragic Sunday of December 1989, Sadai Sadygly found himself in humiliating emptiness. And the very worst thing was that in that emptiness, even the holy altar of the Echmiadzin Church seemed to Sadai Sadygly just as dreary as the stage of their theater.

He left the theater with a dulled heart and a shriveled mind.

Dr. Abasaliev Claims That If a Single Candle Were Lit for Every Murdered Armenian, the Radiance of Those Candles Would Outshine the Moon

A thick fog, enveloping the world entirely. . .

But the world can't consist of fog alone. There's bound to be something behind it. What's hidden in fog is bound to appear soon. Sadai Sadygly knew that, and in his unconscious state he was waiting for just that.

By degrees the fog really did begin to disperse; however, the artist still was unable to understand where he was. And suddenly he found himself on cold stone pavement. And it seemed to him that he was in Aylis, sitting right there in the middle of the little paved stone street leading to the Vuragyrd Church. However, from where he sat the church wasn't visible—not even the high mountain behind the church was visible—and the artist, stricken with anxiety and fear, again attempted to understand where he was: if this were really the little paved Vuragyrd street of Aylis, then where had the church and the mountain gone?

And then, with sweet hope, the artist believed that he was already a long way from mountain and church and the Vuragyrd street and was already approaching Echmiadzin. This new happiness gripped him in precisely that moment when they wheeled him from the operating room to his room, pouring balm into his heart. Although his mind now lacked the strength to understand what was happening, Sadai Sadygly had experienced the change of place with some organ of the senses.

Only on the fourth day, close to evening, did the patient's condition become somewhat better. He wasn't yet able to speak, but it seemed he heard voices and even understood what was being said. For three days Azada *khanum* had been constantly beside her husband. Munavver *khanum* also spent the better part of the day in Sadai Sadygly's room.

And it seemed that Dr. Farzani had found a long-lost kindred spirit in the person of Azada *khanum*. He spent all his spare time in the room. Alternating between Russian and Azeri, they talked to one another on various subjects. The room where Dr. Farzani had placed the artist only four days ago had changed from a hospital space into a home where a friendly family lived.

Azada *khanum* still hadn't brought herself to tell her father about the grave condition of her husband. And while the patient was still in a coma, she asked Dr. Farzani not to disclose the full truth in telephone conversations with her father, as she was afraid it might agitate him.

Dr. Farzani didn't allow anyone except Nuvarish Karabakhly to see the patient. If it had been up to Munavver *khanum*, she wouldn't have allowed Nuvarish, either; she didn't like the fact that Nuvarish always left the room with tears in his eyes. In the nurse's opinion, his tragic pose at the patient's bedside was suggestive of mourning for someone already dead.

On the fourth day of Sadai Sadygly's stay in the hospital, significant changes in his condition began to take place. He moved his tongue, trying to lick his lips. His right hand was in constant movement. The artist was straining every nerve trying to lift it, and Azada *khanum* very much feared this; it seemed to her that he wanted to lift his hand to make the sign of the cross.

Munavver *khanum* fed the patient meat bouillon from a spoon. Dr. Farzani was pacing noiselessly around the room, sometimes stopping and, not taking his eyes off the television, thinking seriously about something. The volume of the television had been turned down; on the screen was some fleshy, round-faced man with a thick beard who'd often been onscreen recently, talking about something heatedly and waving his hands.

As a matter of fact, it was the poet formerly known as Khalilullakh Khalilov who, thanks to his verses about the Party and Lenin, had occupied a place in school readers for more than thirty years. However, in a single year those verses had been erased from people's memories along with the name of their author. Today the poet was called Ulurukh Turanmekan, and hundreds of thousands of people—not only in rallies on Lenin Square but at weddings and funeral feasts in the remotest villages—inspiredly recited his poem "Karabakh—you're my *chyrakh*" from memory. It goes without saying that Dr. Farzani knew absolutely nothing about either Khalilullakh Khalilov or Ulurukh Turanmekan. It's possible that as a doctor, he simply wanted to understand from which sources that person drew his irrepressible energy. In the end, however, he came to the conclusion that there was nothing that needed special understanding here. And two lines addressed to Armenians nudged him towards that conclusion, two lines that the poet pronounced loudly and with special pathos in concluding his performance:

> *Don't you covet my homeland, hai,*
> *We don't share land like a piece of pie.*

"Well, wonderful!" Dr. Farzani waved his hand and, walking away from the television, began pacing around the room again. "That baby with a beard probably isn't even afraid of Azrail. He thinks the day won't arrive when they'll measure out his piece of earth, too. Six feet and a half, at most, and not more than two feet wide. Then again, no," laughed the doctor, "his portion will probably be a bit bigger—his beard is exceedingly wide."

Thus, in an excellent mood, the doctor went up to the patient. He cautiously lifted the eyelids, looking attentively into the pupils.

"For now, the same treatment plan" he said. "We'll wait until he begins to recognize people and speak. We have to do everything to prevent a stroke. If he's able to avoid a stroke, with God's help he'll recover from all the other injuries. For the time being, he's far away. He'll come back when he wants to see us. And if he doesn't want to. . ." The doctor sighed and smiled. "No, God willing, he'll want to."

Sadai Sadygly really was far away. Very far away from the doctor, his wife, the room in which he lay, and even from the trauma to his brain and the wounds to his body. In Aylis. Yes, yes, undoubtedly, he was in Aylis. However, this Aylis wasn't the one that really existed in the world but a living memory of the world Sadai had known when he was four or five, where one spring a beautiful black fox cub had come running from somewhere. Sadai saw him once on the fence of their yard. The black fox cub sprang from the fence to a tree, began to jump from branch to branch, and was lost among the green leaves. And a few days later, Sadai saw how Jinn-Eye Shaban shot that fox cub on the fence in front of the Stone Church near the spring. Since that time, Sadai had dreamed of the fox cub almost every night.

And look, now that fox cub was alive again! Springing from the fences to the trees, from the trees to the fences, he moved from one end of Aylis to the other. And God alone knows how long the little boy of four or five followed the trail of that beautiful black fox cub. He'd never seen a more beautiful animal. And there'd never been a better spring, and there'd never in the world been an Aylis more wonderful than this one. Light. Light all around. On the mountains, sunlight. On the trees, the light of cherries. The first young leaves had just appeared on the willows. The lilacs had just bloomed. What was it about that year, what kind of season was that spring? Because cherries don't ripen at the same time that lilacs flower!

And it also seemed that the fences on which that playful fox cub jumped weren't made of stone but of yellow-rose light, and that light was spilling from the walls onto the streets, the roads. All the yards that the little boy saw in Aylis were neatly cleaned and planted with flowers, and the streets were as clean as freshly cleaned glass.

Colored with that light, water was flowing in the irrigation canals, along the sides of which grew violets and iris. Rejoicing and playing, the handsome fox cub was jumping along the fences, higher, towards the Stone Church, whose cupola was turning gold under the sun's rays. The bright-green leaves of the nut tree, the cherry plum, the apricots growing along the fences and the edges of the irrigation canals were rejoicing and quivering with him. Sometimes the fox cub disappeared from view among the bright-green leaves and then appeared again. And it was in these moments—between the appearance and disappearance of the fox cub—that Sadai Sadygly, lying in the hospital bed, experienced the most painful torment.

In a nutshell, Dr. Farzani's assessment that the patient was now far away was exactly right. And the doctor was also right when he said that now it depended only on the patient himself as to whether he'd continue to live or not. If he wanted to, he'd return; if he didn't want to, he'd remain where he was. . .

For the time being, the patient didn't want to return. The fantastical, wonderful chase after the fox cub continued. And the little boy's sole desire was to catch him, clasp him to his breast, kiss him, and stroke the head and tail of that wonderful creature. While that fox cub was jumping along the fences flooded with light and able to hide among the green leaves—alive and healthy—our artist Sadai Sadygly was also alive.

———

On the last day of the year, the first thing Munavver *khanum* did on coming to work was to remove the patient's bandages. She joyfully told the doctor that the dislocations on two fingers, the left elbow, and the wrist had fully healed. Then Munavver *khanum* and Azada *khanum*, working together, wiped the artist's body with alcohol. Now the broken right leg encased in a cast was the only remaining physical problem. As far as the patient's consciousness, no special changes had been observed; it was still impossible to know whether he was responding to the conversations of those around him.

Azada *khanum* had earlier planned to arrange a New Year's feast in the room. She also invited her father to come from Mardakan and spend the evening with them. Because neither Dr. Farzani nor Munavver *khanum* had anyone with whom to greet the New Year.

However, although he'd promised earlier in the day to come to the city towards evening, Dr. Abasaliev later reconsidered. Long before evening arrived, he phoned and said, "I'm afraid to leave the dacha unguarded on such a day. They've turned the country into a den of bandits. I can't even count on the Mardakanians anymore."

For the first time in her life, Azada *khanum* greeted the New Year without her father. Munavver *khanum*, who lived not far from the hospital, celebrated the New Year along with Azada *khanum* and then went home. Dr. Farzani glanced into the room for a few minutes before Munavver *khanum* left and then sat in his office to wait for a call from his daughter in Moscow. Azada *khanum* remained alone with her husband and, wanting to rouse him, spoke words to him that she'd hidden for long years in the deepest corners of her heart; now, with these words, she caressed her husband like a child. But Sadai Sadygly didn't say a single word that night. Only the eyes of the artist spoke. At times it seemed those eyes laughed, at times it seemed they wept. But most often they were fixed on some endless distance—as if he were looking right at the face of the Almighty.

Early on the morning of the tenth day after Sadai Sadygly had landed in the hospital, Dr. Abasaliev unexpectedly threw open the door and entered the room. When the old psychiatrist appeared on the threshold in a sweater, dressed in a thick jacket, briefcase in hand, Dr. Farzani was washing his hands in the far corner of the room, having just finished his morning rounds. Munavver *khanum* had prepared breakfast for the doctor and laid it out on the little round table. Azada *khanum* was standing at the window and looking at the door thinking about her father, whom she hadn't been able to visit the previous week. And the patient was lying as before, smiling like a little boy of four or five, however, with melancholy reflected in his eyes. . . The day was clear and sunny in spite of a strong wind. A stranger looking in from the outside might have thought that the patient rejoiced more than anyone else at the sunlight now pouring into the room.

Not even removing his jacket, Dr. Abasaliev threw himself on his son-in-law, kissing him. Then he went up to Dr. Farzani and heartily shook his hand, and he familiarly stroked the grey hair of Munavver *khanum*. And only after that did he remove his jacket, throw it on one of the chairs, kiss his daughter on the forehead, and sit in an armchair next to the bed.

Dr. Farzani was astounded; either he was staggered by the liveliness and dash of an acquaintance no longer young, or else it had occurred to him how psychologically healthy the professor was in allowing himself to behave so expressively in the presence of a very ill patient. However, Professor Abasaliev didn't give the doctor the chance to say a word and didn't try to understand the meaning of the secret anxiety in his daughter's eyes. With hands that shook from excitement, the great patriot of Aylis opened the briefcase resting on his knees, pulled a single page from a stack of papers covered in writing and, waving it like a flag, said with unprecedented enthusiasm, "Young man, I've brought you the wonderful Aylis of three hundred and forty years ago! And don't think these are fairy tales. Everything that's written here is one-hundred-percent true.

"At one time I told you that a certain Aylis merchant kept a diary. I saw it at Mirza Vahab's some time before the Turks destroyed Aylis. And after the Second World War, my friend from Yerevan sent me a Russian translation of that diary. I'd forgotten where I hid it, and I looked for it a long time. And think, just recently I found it among some old books. In Russian it's called *The Diary of Zakary Akulissky*.[5] But it seems to me that his name shouldn't be Akulissky but Agulissky. Because in many old books the ancient name of our town is written not as Akulis with a *k* but Agulis with a *g*. Maybe the Russians changed the *g* to *k* later. And in Aylis, you know yourself, to this day they remember that man as Zakary Aylisli. And Mirza Vahab always pronounced the name that way. And my late father knew a lot about him." Dr. Abasaliev transferred his gaze from the patient to Farzani. "Farid, he was so well respected in Aylis that even Muslims name their children in his honor!" He turned again to his son-in-law. "Young man, did you ever, in any other place, see Muslims who gave their sons the name Zakary? And in Aylis you encountered our fellow villager Zakary more often than I did. Do you remember, when we were there, how he went and bought himself a gramophone? He had all of one recording—Khan Shushinsky. He sang 'Who Will Caress You, My Dear, Who Will Caress You, My Dear?' from morning to night."

Seeing that Dr. Farzani was getting ready to leave the room, the professor broke off for a minute. "Where are you going? Sit, listen!" And when the surgeon sat down, he continued, "He wrote in the diary that he was born in 1630. See, that Aylis Armenian recorded everything with German precision, including the day and hour of

his birth *on Sunday, the day of St. Gevorg, in the second half of the day.*"
He pulled still another sheet from his briefcase. "And here's how he
began to trade: on March 5, 1647, at age seventeen, he left Aylis with
a bale of silk. *Today I, Zakary, am leaving Aylis. Holy Spirit, help me!
If I see anything interesting anywhere, I'll write it in my notebook. And
if anyone beholds lies in my writing, may the Holy Spirit enlighten his
reason.*

"Notice he doesn't say 'give him reason' but 'enlighten his
reason.' How noble that man was! Now, pay attention to the route
his travels took: Yerevan, Kars, Erzurum, Tokat, Bursa, Izmir, and
later Stambul. And he always writes not 'Stambul' but 'Stambol.' His
first journey lasted ten months; at the end of December, he returns
to Aylis. After that, where didn't he go? Greece, Venice, Spain,
Portugal, Germany, Poland, Holland. . ."

Azada *khanum* poured her father a little hot tea in place of
the cold.

"Drink just a glass of tea," she said. "Your Armenian merchant
isn't running off anywhere."

"I already had tea. You know I only drink tea once a day," Dr.
Abasaliev answered his daughter angrily, and in that same angry
tone he continued, "Do you know how much misery those sheikhs,
khans, and sultans brought Aylis?! Here, listen, I'll read: *July 10,
1653, Aylis. Today Aga Liatif, the deputy of Sheikh Abbas, arrived in
Aylis. He wrote down the names of sixteen young boys and girls on a
paper but didn't take anyone with him. This time God spared us.*

"And how many misfortunes Sheikh Suleiman, the successor of
Sheikh Abbas, rained down on Aylis! *Someone by the name of Gagaiyz
Bey arrived in Aylis today from Yerevan on the order of Safikuli Khan.
He led thirty horsemen with him. By order of the sheikh, they had to
collect one thousand tomans from the inhabitants of Aylis. There was no
limit to the bribe taking, oppression, and violence. They subjected more
than one hundred people to torture and hung thirty-five people. But even
after all that suffering, the people could only collect 350 tomans in all.*"

Not only had Dr. Abasaliev translated the diary from Russian into Azeri—the diary of that Armenian merchant who'd been born three hundred and forty years earlier in Aylis and who'd traveled the whole world—but it seemed he'd learned the whole text by heart. The extraordinary memory of this person who was already more than eighty years old struck Dr. Farzani. He followed his colleague attentively and heard him with growing interest.

"*Today Khosrov Aga arrived in Aylis and announced to the people that he'd been named ruler of Gokhtan. He led many people from Merga, Shorut, Legram—that's what they called Negram earlier. How they mocked the rich Aylis landowner Ovanes. They sat the poor fellow on a donkey and had him carried all around to the sound of the zurna. Then they took one hundred tomans from him and let him go.*"

Dr. Abasaliev sorted through the papers in his briefcase for a short while. "Just think, young man," he said. "Can you imagine, on July 22, 1669, snow fell in Aylis! And in 1677 there was not a drop of rain from the third of June through the end of August. And in May of 1680 such a downpour broke out that it washed away all the houses by the river. And later there was such a drought that nowhere from Nakhchivan to Tabriz was there water, not even to drink. In 1667 more than two hundred children perished from smallpox in Aylis. In 1679 there was such a strong earthquake in Yerevan that walls cracked in the houses and churches even in Aylis. Zakary Agulissky lists all the churches in Aylis. The Vang Church is the church of Saint Foma. You know that. Vuragyrd is a corrupted form of the word Vardakert, and the Vuragyrd Church where you and I walked is the Church of Saint Christopher. And the church we call the Stone Church is the Church of Saint Ovanes—it seems it was built during Zakary Agulissky's time. Or else it was restored during that time and reopened on November 5, 1665. That's what it says in the diary."

Again Dr. Abasaliev rummaged for a while among his papers. "*January 4, 1668. Today there was an earthquake in Aylis. . . February*

26, 1668. Today a comet appeared over Aylis in the western half of the sky. It foretells misfortune for our sins... December 21, 1668. Archimandrite Petros, head of the Monastery of Saint Foma, commanded that the monastery be enclosed on all sides with a tall fence. They are using river stone and baked brick to construct the cupolas and bell tower. Master builders arrived from Kurdistan—at that time the Turkish regions of Van, Bitlis, and Diyarbakır were called Kurdistan. *The interior walls are being faced with stone. Water is being conveyed to the monastery. God grant strength to all the builders.*"

Dr. Abasaliev was no longer looking at the patient; one after the other, he pulled pages covered with writing from his briefcase and read them with strange passion, as if for himself.

Understanding that this might go on for some time, Munavver *khanum* tried to interrupt. "But, Doctor, people are writing all over the place that those churches aren't Armenian but Albanian. They say the Armenians claimed them later. Perhaps your Zakary wasn't Armenian but Albanian?"

It seems that Dr. Abasaliev didn't want to take even a second to raise his head and look at the nurse. Not lifting his eyes from the paper, he exclaimed, "You're talking complete nonsense! If someone calls himself an Armenian, how can I say: 'No, you're not Armenian? You're an Albanian or a Lezgin, a Talysh, a Multanets.' It's true that the language of the Aylis Armenians differs a little bit from the language of the Yerevan Armenians. And a difference is noticeable in the writing. But you know, in our Ordubad every Muslim village speaks its own dialect. You'd never confuse people from Shaki with those from Baku—there's so much difference in language, character, and customs. It's the same way with Armenians. I don't know who those Albanians were or where they lived. But I do know that the people in Aylis were Armenians. Moreover, the very best kind of Armenians.

"Yes," said the doctor, again addressing Farid Farzani, "after the Arab invasion—from the eighth through the thirteenth centuries—

there were Turkish and Tatar-Mongolian invasions and the Oghuz and Seljuks. Then, for almost three centuries that land was the arena for bloody wars between Iran and Turkey. One group arrives, kills, then the other arrives, kills. If a single candle were lit for every murdered Armenian, the radiance of those candles would outshine the moon. The Armenians endured it all, but they never agreed to change their faith. Those people were worn out and tormented by violence, but they never stopped building their churches, writing their books, and raising their hands to the heavens, calling on their God."

"And what else can a people who lack land do? Just stay put, call on the heavens!" answered Farid Farzani, chuckling quietly.

Dr. Abasaliev pulled out yet another sheet from his stack. "*October 7, 1651. Tabriz. I arrived in Tabriz with my brother Simon. The ruler of Tabriz, Aligulu Khan, wanted Simon to convert to the Muslim faith. Only God saved us from that great misfortune.* That's how piously our Agulis natives believed in their God, Farid. You know, Aligulu Khan was prepared to shower Simon with gold if he'd agree to accept the Muslim religion." He looked at the patient, who was smiling continuously, smiled broadly and heartily himself, and continued speaking with his earlier fervor. "The Armenians had a wild poet—Yegishe Charents—who was purged in 1937. They say that restless merrymaker and great lover of strong mulberry vodka once joked quite wittily, 'We didn't let them cut one pitiful piece of unnecessary skin from a certain place, and it gave them a remarkably slick excuse to cut an entire nation to pieces.'"

There still remained a half-hour until the patient was administered his regular round of medicine. However, Azada *khanum*, recognizing that her father was going to continue reading the diaries, walked towards the bed and began to make signs to him; she meant, It's time to leave the patient in peace. And once again, the doctor paid no attention to his daughter's worry. He pulled a new page from his briefcase and, waving it, said, "And what's written here, young man! Look, on November 10, 1676, Zakary Agulissky writes: *I, Zakary, planted a large, spreading plane tree in the yard of the Church of Saint Ovanes today.* It seems to me there wasn't any plane tree there by the Stone Church. But maybe one does grow there, I've forgotten: you know better than I do."

And at that moment Sadai Sadygly's eyes suddenly opened unbelievably wide, and he muttered with shaking lips:

"Chesh-me-se-din! Ech-ma-echmaz-za!"

Those were the first sounds resembling a word that he'd spoken the whole time he'd spent in the hospital bed. But only Azada *khanum* was able to understand that they meant "Echmiadzin." And understanding that, she couldn't help herself: sobbing loudly, she burst piteously into tears.

"Papa! Papa!" she said through sobs. "He still can't speak, Papa! He doesn't know anyone. And you talk, talk, talk without stopping."

Dr. Abasaliev instantly turned white. As if he were a person who'd been suddenly awakened and was trying hard to understand where he was, he looked at the patient and then in turn at Farzani, at Munavver *khanum*, and at his only daughter weeping uncontrollably.

"But he said something just now," said the professor, looking with piteous inquiry at Farzani.

"Yes, it seems he produced some sounds. He should have spoken long ago. But for some reason, it's taking a long time."

"Clearly, he has a heavy kind of amnesia. Why didn't you say anything to me earlier?"

"Well, you didn't let us open our mouths," answered Dr. Farzani with a bit of friendly reproach. "You were far away, you ran off to Aylis three hundred years ago and didn't even notice us!" Dr. Farzani laughed and then asked in a more serious tone, "Doctor, were all those people really in Aylis?"

"Of course they were! In those times people lived in Aylis who were the equals of gods. They channeled water, planted gardens, hewed stones. Those Armenians, both artisans and traders, went around and visited hundreds of strange cities and villages, earn-ing money bit by bit just so they could turn every shred of earth of their little Agulis into a heavenly place. Ever since the Turks departed at the end of 1919, leaving Aylis in ruins, to this day the Muslim population looks for gold in the ruins of Armenian homes. Even when they plow the earth to sow crops, they hope for—look, look!—pure gold to turn up under their feet. The same gold that helped the Armenians extract water from under the earth and hew carriage highways from all directions in the mountains. They built a weir. Along the banks of the river, they erected a parapet from hewn river stones. They paved all the streets with choice river cobblestones. Over time, twelve majestic churches were also built in Aylis with that gold. Perhaps a ton of gold was spent on each of them."

From his faraway world, the patient gazed at Dr. Abasaliev with unceasing astonishment. This person seemed to Sadai Sadygly like someone he knew, and the artist was trying with all his might to remember who he was. The women waited impatiently for the end of the conversation about churches, monks, and Aylis.

Munavver *khanum* spoke about the patient's condition. "His wounds healed quickly, Doctor," she said, addressing Abasaliev. "There was a dislocation in one arm, several fingers were dislocated in several places, but over four or five days everything healed. And the knee fracture isn't dangerous. He moves his toes easily. His system is still young and will mend quickly, God willing. There could have been complications after a concussion. You know that better than anyone. And ten days is a long time, Doctor. In that amount of time, the patient should at least have been able to speak. Perhaps he should be sent to Moscow before it's too late. Farid Gasanovich and Azada *khanum* think so, too."

"It's amnesia in the form of confabulation. In psychiatry we also call this Korsakoff's syndrome Did you conduct an angiogram?" Abasaliev asked Dr. Farzani.

"A craniography was done yesterday. We don't have angiography equipment." Dr. Farzani was silent a little while and added, "Munavver *khanum* is right, it would be better to send him to Moscow."

"And what did the craniography show?"

"Nothing good," answered Dr. Farzani, and after a little thought he added, "I noticed a small tumor in his brain. Perhaps it's an old tumor, it's hard to say now. At the moment it's very dangerous to move the patient; it's necessary to wait a little while. However, I don't think we'll be able to manage this without Moscow." Glancing at Azada *khanum*, he hung his head guiltily.

For a little while, no one uttered a sound. Dr. Abasaliev broke the silence, communicating one more piece of unpleasant news.

"Azia, did you hear what that Nuvarish did?"

"No, what did he do?"

"They say he threw himself off a balcony."

"Who says that?" whispered Azada, her voice shaking.

"Women were talking in the bakery in Mardakan. And I myself heard about his death three or four days ago on the radio. But I didn't know he killed himself."

"So that's why he stopped coming here," said Dr. Farzani.

"Allah rest his soul," muttered Munavver *khanum*, her whole body rocking sorrowfully.

Dr. Abasaliev, who that morning had appeared in the room inspired, left the hospital around noon completely changed and went home to Mardakan.

And Sadai existed as before in his faraway world. Now the little boy following the beautiful black fox cub was at the top of the hill that divided the upper and lower quarters of the village and not far from the Stone Church nestled up to the slope of the mountain that was a little rose-colored in the rays of the sun. The air was full of the thick, bitter aroma of the leaves of the nut trees mixed with cool water, because the green branches of the walnut trees from all around leaned towards the height where he stood. The sound of the water seething in the stone reservoir beneath the Stone Church resounded far and wide.

And the beautiful black fox cub kept jumping between the green branches. The little boy was afraid to lose sight of him, but at the same time he wanted a drink. His brain was burning with thirst. And the cool water running loudly in the ditch laid of stone and coursing into the little stone pool was attracting him to itself like a magnet. But fear of losing the fox cub wouldn't let him go near it.

Then he saw the fox cub spring from a tree to the stone fence and continue his journey. The little boy rejoiced: now he could come closer to the ringing water. He put his palm under its resilient stream. However, not a single drop of water landed in the little boy's palm. He didn't feel the slightest coolness, quite the opposite—he was enveloped in nauseatingly hot air. The little boy thrust his head into the ditch to cool his burning brain. But here, too, nothing happened—even that energetic water couldn't cool a brain engulfed in flame. At precisely that moment, fear enveloped the little boy, fear he'd lose sight of the black fox cub forever. And just then a shot rang out. The whistle of the flying bullet burst like molten lead in the artist's ears. Trying to understand where the shot had come from, he gathered all his strength, and lifting his head, in place of the stone fences woven of light he saw the ordinary, grey fence molded of clay of today's Aylis and the scarlet blood of the wonderful, furry, coal-black fox cub of his childhood flowing across it.

Blood was still flowing across the fence when the hum that had for a long time roamed like a swarm of bees through the chinks of the cracked walls of the Aylis churches rose like a black cloud in the sky, mixing with the sound of the shot.

Before closing his eyes forever, high, high under Heaven, on the slope of the tallest mountain of Aylis, he suddenly saw the Vuragyrd Church clearly—the "Pigeon Bazaar." And he finally understood that there was nowhere further for him to go.

On Friday, January 12, 1990, evening approached.

Crying out frightening slogans about freedom, independence, and Karabakh, Ulurukh Turanmekan had led a neurasthenic crowd of unmarried women through the streets all day. Now, towards evening, he conducted yet another rally by the Armenian church located next to the Parapet. Khalilullakh's assistants had already been trying for more than an hour to set it on fire. However, the church simply didn't want to burn, and it was this circumstance that especially enraged the unmarried women-patriots surrounding the poet.

In the hospital car, Azada *khanum* and Munavver *khanum* conveyed Sadai Sadygly's body to the mosque for the ritual of washing.

Not having been able to save the patient from stroke, the sad and miserable Dr. Farzani sat in his office, for the first time feeling himself alien and transitory there. Mentally bidding a final farewell to Baku, that evening he waited for the call from his Moscow daughter with especially agitated hope and especially anxious worry.

The clouds of black smoke coming from the windows of the church near the Parapet became thicker and thicker, mixing with the black night of January 13, 1990, which smelled of blood.

At home in Mardakan, Dr. Abasaliev knew nothing about any of it yet.

And the pigeons spending the night in the Aylis churches still slept peacefully and dreamed pigeon dreams.

Aylis, July 2006
Baku, June 2007

Glossary of Terms

arvad: A wife. Used as a polite way of addressing a married woman.

babki: A game of ancient origin played by throwing animal bones or other small objects.

bey: A courtesy title for men.

chyrakh: A sanctuary.

dacha: A country cottage used by urban dwellers, especially in the summer. During the Soviet period, the government distributed dachas only among prominent Communist Party members and the newly created academic and cultural elite. Towards the end of the Soviet era, dachas became more accessible to the middle class.

gardash: A brother. Used as a polite way of addressing a person of the same age.

hai: The Armenian term for one's Armenian nationality.

hajji: A person who has completed the *haj* to Mecca.

khanum: A respectful way of addressing a woman of high social status derived from the feminine equivalent of the male title *khan*.

khash: A dish of boiled cow or sheep parts.

kishi: A man. Used as a polite way of addressing an older man.

Komsomol: The All-Union Leninist Young Communist League, or Young Communist League, was a Soviet political organization that helped instill Communist values in young people. Its members received social, political, and (during *perestroika*) even commercial advantages throughout the Soviet period; many members went on to hold positions of power in the Soviet government.

lavash: A soft, thin, oven-baked, unleavened flatbread eaten all over the Caucasus and Western Asia.

muallim: A teacher. Used as a polite way of addressing a professor.

nomenkla-tura: The privileged class of government managers and bureaucrats under the Soviet system of government. Almost all were members of the Communist Party.

papakha: A wool hat worn by men in the Caucasus.

perestroika: The official government policy of reforming and restructuring political and economic realities during the last decade of the Soviet era. The policy was most closely associated with the leadership of Mikhail Gorbachev.

qanat: A type of underground irrigation canal.

saj: A special kind of frying pan.

sary: An Azeri word meaning "light-haired."

shor: A salty curd cheese.

shorpa: A rich meat and vegetable soup or stew.

sujug Fruit sausage stuffed with nuts.

toman: A Persian monetary unit, used also in Azerbaijan briefly after the Second World War.

yerazy: An abbreviation meaning "Yerevan Azerbaijanis," ethnic Azeri refugees from Armenia.

zurna: A woodwind instrument used to play folk music.

Notes

1 *Majnun and Layla* is a love story, originally in Arabic, set in pre-Islamic Hejaz, concerning the love of the seventh-century Bedouin poet Qays ibn Al-Mulawwah (known in the story as *majnun*, meaning "madman" in Arabic, Persian, and Azeri) for Layla. The most influential version of the story was the Persian version of the poet Nizami of Ganja (present-day Azerbaijan) in 1188. As a result of this story, the word *majnun* became synonymous with an extreme form of romantic love in Islamic culture. [Series editor's note]

2 This is a humorous verse that actually exists in Aylis folklore; it's not intended to be spiteful. [Author's note]

3 These lines are lightly paraphrased from the play *Vagif* by [Soviet Azeri poet] Samed Vurgun (1906–1956). In their original language, the lines rhyme sonorously. [Russian editor's note]

4 Caucasian Albania refers to an ancient territory (4th BCE–8th century CE) that overlapped with present day Azerbaijan and southern Daghestan. It was a multiethnic region that had its own language (related to Udi, a modern language indigenous to the northeast Caucasus) as well as Middle Persian. [Series editor's note]

5 *The Diary of Zakary Akulissky* was published by the Academy of Sciences of the Armenian SSR in Yerevan in 1939. All citations are from this edition of the diary. [Russian editor's note]

Akram Aylisli is an Azerbaijani writer, playwright, novelist, and editor. His works have been translated from his native Azeri into more than 20 languages. For decades, he was one of the most well-regarded writers in Azerbaijan. His books were taught at schools, and he was awarded the official title of People's Writer in 1998, as well as two of the highest state awards, the Shokrat and Istiglal medals. From 2005 to 2010, he served as a deputy in Azerbaijan's national assembly. The 2012 publication of his novella *Stone Dreams* led to book burnings and the continuous harassment of the author himself. Since 2016 he has lived under a politically motivated criminal investigation and corresponding restrictions on his activities in Baku, Azerbaijan.

Katherine E. Young is the author of the poetry collections *Woman Drinking Absinthe* and *Day of the Border Guards* and the editor of *Written in Arlington*. She is the translator of work by Anna Starobinets (memoir), Akram Aylisli (fiction), and numerous Russophone poets. Young was named a 2017 National Endowment for the Art translation fellow. From 2016-2018, she served as the inaugural Poet Laureate for Arlington, Virginia.